TRAIL BLAZERS

When a trail was needed to supply the meat-starved North and East, Gregg Halmar, veteran of the Civil War, was chosen as Trail Blazer. Pushing through deserts and Indian territory meant facing a constant gamble with death. For a thousand miles, Halmar led the cattle to the North, fighting outlaws, Indians and nature. It was men like Halmar who turned the West into what it is today; who rode each day on the thin edge of danger . . .

E. C. TUBB

TRAIL BLAZERS

Complete and Unabridged

LINFORD
Leicester

First published in Great Britain in 2000

Gloucestershire County Council	

British Library CIP Data

Tubb, E. C.
    Trail blazers.—Large print ed.—
Linford western library
1. Western stories
2. Large type books
I. Title
823.9'14 [F]

ISBN 978–1–84617–968–6

Published by
F. A. Thorpe (Publishing)
Anstey, Leicestershire

Set by Words & Graphics Ltd.
Anstey, Leicestershire
Printed and bound in Great Britain by
T. J. International Ltd., Padstow, Cornwall

This book is printed on acid-free paper

1

The house was in a little alley running from the central plaza. A dingy place with high barred windows and a narrow door splotched with the grille of a Judas window. A smell hung around it, the stale odour of wine and indifferent cooking, the reek of garbage and the raw scent of tequila. Two Indian boys hung around outside, their eyes searching the filth of the alley for anything of value. A soldier walked down the alley, neat in his blue uniform, his pistol holster and boots polished until they shone, his sabre jingling at his side. He glanced at the two boys and they shuffled away from his approach.

Gregg Halmar did not move. He leaned against the wall, stuck a cigarette in his mouth and stooped over a spluttering match.

A big man, this Halmar. Tough with a

face chipped from granite and blue eyes like flecks of ice. His mouth was a thin, hard streak above a strong jaw, and the knuckles of both hands were scarred. He wore farm clothes, patched jeans and a torn flannel shirt, broken boots and a frayed jacket which hugged broad shoulders. He sucked smoke into his lungs and watched the soldier from beneath the shadow of a battered hat.

The man glanced at him casually, without any real interest, not really seeing him or, if he did, dismissing him for just another poor white, a transient labourer, one of the thousands of men who were pressing into the West from the wreck of the Civil War.

He was wrong.

Gregg waited until the man had left the alley, striding from the shadows into the hot, New Mexican sun, then crossed the street and rapped on the door of the house. He waited, knocked again, then, as no answer came, kicked with his broken boots at the thick panelling. Hinges creaked as the Judas window swung open and eyes, glittering in the semi-darkness of the interior, stared at him.

'What is it?' The words were Spanish, spoken by a woman no longer young.

'Let me in.' said Halmar in the same tongue. 'I am to see Pedro.'

'Pedro?' There was doubt in the voice. 'I know no one of that name.'

'Pedro Lopez,' said Halmar. 'He knows me. Let me in, fast!'

The Judas window slammed and soft footsteps shuffled in the distance. Gregg stood waiting, dragging at his cigarette, trying to control his impatience. He had waited a long time for this moment, he could afford to wait a little longer.

After what seemed to be a long time the footsteps returned, the door swung open with a creak of hinges, and Gregg stepped into the interior.

A woman stared at him from where she had shut the door. A swarthy Mexican, her hair in lank strands about her face, her dress dirty and spotted with grease. She jerked her head towards the flight of stairs.

'He will see you.'

'Now?'

'Later.' She produced a bottle of tequila and a glass.

'It is the time of the siesta, Pedro is resting.' Glass touched glass and tequila gurgled. 'A drink, *señor*?'

'*Gracias*.' Gregg took the glass, lifted it to his mouth, tilted it, swallowed the raw spirit. The woman silently refilled the glass.

'Pedro is upstairs, you say?'

'Yes.'

'Does he know that I am here?'

'I told him, *señor*. He ordered me to give you a drink and make you comfortable.'

'That was nice of him.' Gregg drank again, the tequila making his mood ugly. 'Tell him to quit horsing around. I've come a long away to see him and I don't aim to wait. Tell him that if he doesn't come down pronto, I'm coming up. Tell him that.'

The woman nodded, not arguing, and shuffled upstairs. Alone, Gregg began to punish the bottle. He had come a long way, and eaten little, and lived in a state of nervous tension. By the time the woman returned he had killed half the bottle and felt the need for action.

The woman had returned alone. Impatiently he brushed past her and mounted the stairs. Four doors opened on a landing and he hesitated, trying to decide which to open first. A man coughed and Gregg stepped forward, flinging open the door.

Pedro Lopez was a runt of a man. He had a thin, rat-like face with a scar, the relic of a knife fight, tracing its path across one cheek from the corner of his left eye to the point of his jaw. He wore bright clothing, high boots, spurs, a leather jacket. Around his waist a broad leather belt studded with cartridges held a holstered Colt and a long-bladed knife. The hilt of the knife and the butt of the Colt were both of ivory ornamented with silver. Silver coins were sewed to his jacket, belt, chaps and boots.

He stared at Gregg, one thin hand touching the butt of his gun, then as he recognized the big man he smiled and relaxed.

'Gregg! It is good to see you once more.'

'Your welcome overwhelms me,' said Gregg drily. He stared around the room. A pair of saddlebags rested on the table and from the window Gregg could see a saddle horse at the hitch-rail. A sloping roof led from the window to a few feet above the street. He stared at Lopez.

'If I were a suspicious man,' he said slowly, 'I'd think that you were trying to stall me so as to make a getaway.'

'The horse?' Pedro shrugged, his white teeth flashing in his brown face. 'A precaution, my friend, that is all. A wise man sees to it that he has two ways out of every situation.' He gestured with his slender hands. 'But come, this is no way to meet. Maria! Bring wine and food and tequila for my friend.' He smiled again. 'She is fat, that one, but her cooking!' He made a gesture. 'So different from the last time we ate together.'

'I'm glad you remember that,' said Gregg. He held out his hand. 'Give.'

'Your money.' Pedro smiled again. 'Is that it?'

'That's it.' Gregg stared at the swarthy Mexican. 'I'm glad you haven't tried to deny it.'

'Why should I?' Pedro shrugged. He reached for a box of cigars, offered them, lit them. Maria came into the room with a tray and bottles and Gregg felt his stomach warm to the sight of food and wine. He put down his cigar and reached for the food.

'How long has it been, my friend?' Pedro puffed smoke towards the flies crawling on the ceiling. 'A year? More? A year, I think.'

'Nine months,' said Gregg. He swallowed, helped himself to wine and reached for the food.

'Nine months.' Pedro chuckled. 'The war was ending. You were a captain in the Confederate Army and I was a scout. You had money, twenty thousand dollars in gold to pay the mercenaries fighting for the South. We were discovered by a Union patrol and had to run for it. Your horse was shot and you were wounded. It seemed that nothing could save the gold from falling into enemy hands.'

Gregg listened, his mouth full, his eyes watchful.

'So I had the great idea. I would take the gold and ride across the border to a trail known only to me. I would hide and wait until the war was over and then I would come north and meet you and we would share the gold. That was what we decided, yes?'

'Yes.'

'You trusted me,' said Pedro. 'But you could do nothing else. I could have shot you and taken the gold. I could have taken the gold and simply disappeared. I could have hidden the gold and told the Union soldiers where you were.'

'That wouldn't have been necessary,' said Gregg. 'They found me.' His face hardened. 'They took me and put me into a hospital which was more like a slaughterhouse than a place for the sick and wounded. They dug out that bullet and left me to live or to die, rot or recover. I fooled them, I lived, so they let me go with an old uniform and nothing else, not even a horse. It took me a long time to work my way to the rendezvous. I waited for weeks trying to get word to you. It was lucky that I managed to trace you here.'

'Good luck for the two of us,' said Pedro. He made a gesture. 'I waited as long as I dare, my friend, but then I had to leave. A little trouble, a gambler who dealt from the bottom, you understand?'

'You shot him,' said Gregg. 'I heard about it.' He pushed away the tray and relit his cigar. 'All right, Pedro, let's get down to it. Where's my share of the money?'

'The money,' said Pedro, and stared out of the window.

'Don't stall.' said Gregg. His hand lifted to the open neck of his shirt. 'I want that money.'

'Of course.' The Mexican shrugged. 'But it isn't as easy as all that, Gregg. I had to spend money to bribe the soldiers, spend more to buy horses. then I had to live and run, and at times fight. It wasn't easy.'

'The money.'

'You shall have what is left,' said Pedro. 'That I promise.' He stared at the big man. 'What will you do with it, Gregg?'

'Buy some decent clothes, a good horse, and live like a man instead of a tramp.' Gregg stared distastefully at his clothing. 'Look at these rags!'

'Better than none,' said Pedro philsophically. He leaned across the table. 'How would you like to make lots of money?'

'I have money,' reminded Gregg. 'You are holding it for me.'

'Aside from that.' Pedro glanced towards the door, rose, shut and locked it, then returned to his seat. He spoke softly, his eyes glinting with enthusiasm.

'Listen, Gregg, I have not been idle. I have looked at the opportunities and they are tremendous. The country has not yet recovered from the war and things are still unsettled. Wagon trains are pressing toward the West to California and Oregon. More, the cattle raisers here in New Mexico and in Texas are loaded with beef. They have increased the size of their herds during the war, when none could be shipped or sold. Some of the ranges have thousands of head of cattle just waiting to be picked up by the right man.' He winked. 'Follow me?'

'Keep talking.'

'We can make some real money. We gather around us a band of desperate men, men willing to ride and shoot and die if they have to, and then we take what we want. The west and south are full of such men. Discharged soldiers, ex-guerrillas, we could get some of Quantrill's men if we tried. Then, when we have them, we can make our fortunes.'

'I see.' Gregg nodded as he thought about it. Pedro was right. The south-west was in the midst of turmoil, and a strong man could make his mark. He looked at the Mexican as he thought of something.

'The Indians?'

'Bad, but we can stay away from them.' Pedro poured wine and lit a fresh cigar. 'This is the plan. We start small and so gain a reputation. We can attack the buffalo hunters' camps. The hide buyers are sure to have plenty of money. We can rob stage coaches of the gold from the mines. We can — '

'We can start by getting some sense,' interrupted Gregg. 'You're talking about starting another war.'

'Well?' Pedro rolled his cigar and stared at the big man. 'Soft, Gregg?'

'Maybe, but I don't aim to go on no killing spree just for a little cash.'

'It's waiting to be picked up,' said Pedro. 'I know a dozen men who would ride with us. Join us and we can ride tomorrow.'

'Maybe.' Gregg frowned at the window. 'How you aim to operate?'

'I told you.'

'You told me pipe-dreams. I don't mean wild talk, I mean a plan. This cattle now, what would you do with it if you had it?'

'Smuggle it over the border.'

'For how much a head?'

Pedro looked blank and Gregg smiled.

'You see? Go your way and you'll be shot down in no time at all. You've got guts, Pedro, I've always known that, but you lack brains. You're a man of action, not thought.'

'You can plan, Gregg. What do you say?'

'Simple. We play it honest.' Gregg shrugged at the expression on the

13

man's face. 'Look at it this way, turn outlaw and the country will rise against you. You'll get by for a time, sure, but you won't sleep easy and you'll die in your boots. I've got a better idea. I met a lot of people on my way here and those people talked. You know the price of beef in Texas? Five dollars a head, that's what. You know what cattle are fetching in Omaha? Forty to fifty dollars a head. Figure out the profit on two thousand head.'

'Eighty thousand dollars,' said Pedro, and licked his lips.

'That's right.' Gregg drew at his cigar. 'And that's taking it low. With real money to spend we could buy cattle at maybe four dollars a head. We can hire cowpunchers at forty a month and found, pay them off when we sell the cattle. We can make ourselves fifty or sixty thousand dollars and stay alive long enough to spend it.'

'But — ' Pedro shook his head.

'But what?'

'But you talk wild, my friend. Texas is

near, yes, but Nebraska is almost a thousand miles away. We would have to cross Oklahoma and Kansas, and Kansas is wild and rough.'

'So?'

'So we'd never get through with our cattle.' Pedro shrugged at Gregg's expression. 'I tell you the truth. Why do you think the Texas herds are still unsold? The ranchers know that they can sell their beef for high prices as well as you do, but they dare not face the drive. They know what will happen to them once they hit the Kansas border. The jayhawks would rob them and take their cattle. They would kill the cowpunchers and stampede the herds.'

'The jayhawks.' Gregg scowled as he thought about them. Rough riders, guerrillas, little more than outlaws, they were men who had fought against Missouri both before and during the Civil War. Now they ranged the border, and under the guise of patriotism levied toll on all strangers who tried to cross the State.

'And there are Indians,' said Pedro. 'Wandering bands from the reservations.'

'Indians can be fought off,' said Gregg. 'And the jayhawks avoided.'

'Only by blazing a new trail.' Pedro leaned back, puffing at his cigar. 'Give up the idea, my friend. Ride with me and gain plenty of money, plenty of food, wine and fine horses. We shall have men to obey and money to burn.'

Gregg shrugged, not answering, and stared out of the window. The hot summer sun seemed to beat down from the sky like the naked coals of hell itself. It was hot, so hot that even the flies rested where they settled, and the only signs of life were a few somnolent Mexicans and a scavenging dog. Down below the tethered horse stamped and pawed the ground in its impatience to be on the move. Gregg stared down at it, noted the silver-studded saddle, the Winchester in the scabbard, the bed-roll and the coiled lariat.

He turned from the window and

stared at the Mexican.

'I'm no outlaw,' he said. 'I don't intend becoming one. The money you took was as much mine as anyone's. If the Union forces had taken it it would have been lost just the same.' He held out his hand. 'Ten thousand dollars, Pedro. Give.'

'You are a fool, Gregg,' said the swarthy man. 'Let me hold the money to buy horses and guns and hire men. We can rule in this part of the world. Over the border the *vaqueros* are ready and waiting for a man with gold to lead them. They will ride like the wind and rob these fools of their money. With the money we can buy more guns, hire more men. Gregg, this is the chance I have been waiting for all my life.'

'Then take it,' Gregg snapped shortly. 'You don't need me.'

'I need your money,' said Pedro, and now he had lost his smile. 'You are a fool, Gregg to trust a man with so much money. Better to have thrown it into a fire.'

'Don't joke with me Pedro,' said Gregg. He took a step closer to the swarthy man, one hand reaching out for the bottle of tequila, the other for a glass. He filled the glass, then paused staring at the Mexican. 'Where is the money?'

'I have it.'

'Give it to me.'

'No.'

'You refuse?' Gregg wasn't surprised, he had expected something like this. Pedro shrugged.

'Be reasonable, my friend. We have spoken of riding and robbing and killing, if need be, for gold. Why should I hesitate at killing you? You are one man, unarmed, without protection or friends. I could kill you and no one would blame me, but I am merciful. I spare your life and take only your gold.' He smiled, his teeth white against his olive skin. 'Accept what life brings, *amigo*. Today you, tomorrow me, who knows?'

Gregg threw the contents of the glass into his face.

He was quick, very quick, but not quick enough. Something, it may have been the tensing of his muscles, warned the Mexican, and he ducked, avoiding the raw spirit flung at his eyes. His hand flashed to his side and, as he rose, the long-barrelled Colt slid from its holster, the hammer clicking back beneath the pressure of his thumb.

Gregg threw the bottle as he fired, jumping to one side. The pistol roared, lead blasting through the air where he had stood; then Pedro swore as the heavy bottle struck his shoulder, numbing it for an instant and throwing him off balance.

He swore again as a hard first slammed against his gun wrist. The blow knocked the Colt from his hand, and before he could recover it Gregg was all over him.

The big man fought with a grim ferocity which had as its aim the desire to win and win as fast as possible. He struck at the olive face, sent his knee into Pedro's stomach, drove his fist against the other's mouth, nose, throat and jaw. The Mexican cursed, clawed at his knife, drew it, sent it forward in a killing thrust. Gregg twisted just in time, the razor steel slitting his shirt and skin, then he struck again, struck with all the pent-up fury of a man who has lived too long in poverty and fading hope.

Pedro grunted, his eyes rolled upwards and, like a falling tree, he crashed to the floor.

Snatching up the Colt, Gregg listened. The shot had apparently attracted little attention, shots were frequent in the frontier towns, and no one outside came to see what was wrong. Maria, the big woman, came wheezing up the stairs, calling as she went.

'What is it? What is wrong?'

'Nothing.' Gregg went to the door, stood there so as to hide Pedro from view. He smiled at the woman.

'Nothing is wrong. It was an accident, Pedro was showing me his pistol and it went off.'

'So.' She stared at him, her eyes bright and glistening with suspicion. 'Where is Pedro?'

'He is well.'

'Where is he?'

'All right.' Gregg stepped forward, the Colt in his hand levelling at the woman. 'Do not scream or call for help. Pedro is not dead, he tried to kill me and I knocked him down.' He stepped to one of the other doors, opened it, looked inside the room. It was a bedroom, and a key rested on the inside of the lock. He gestured with the Colt.

'Inside.'

'But — '

'Inside.' His harsh voice made the soft Spanish seem ominous. He waited until she had passed into the room, removed the key, closed the door and locked her in. Dropping the key he returned to the room where Pedro sprawled on the floor. The little man breathed harshly, his nose broken and streaming blood. Gregg stooped over him, turned him, felt for a money belt. He found it, a double fold of leather, and taking the silver-mounted knife he cut away the shirt from around the little man's waist. The leather buckle of the belt was stiff, and Gregg snarled with impatience as he fumbled with it. Again he used the knife, slitting the tough leather, then, the belt in his hand, he rose and glanced around the room.

The saddle-bags met his eyes.

He examined them, opening the flaps and staring inside. They held coffee, flour, some beans and bacon, and a bottle of tequila. Pedro had been packing for the trail when Gregg had arrived.

He picked up the saddle-bags and stepped to the window. Below him the horse stamped again, still impatient. The horse was the only sign of life, the central plaza was empty, the streets thick with dust and deserted during the heat of the day.

Swiftly Gregg counted the money in the belt, ripping open the leather and spilling out the notes. They were greenbacks, much lighter than gold and far easier to handle. Gregg counted eleven thousand dollars. He thrust the money into his pockets, stared at the silver-mounted gun in his hand, looked at Pedro, unconscious on the floor, and grinned.

'I could take your fancy gun and belt,' he said. 'I could take your knife and steal your horse and gear, but I won't. I'll leave the gun and borrow the horse. I'll send it back from the livery stable in the next town. You can call it even.'

Picking up the saddle-bags he crawled through the window, slid down the roof and dropped to the ground. Throwing the bags over the mount he swung into the saddle and, driving his heels into the horse's flanks, rode across the plaza and towards the edge of the town.

Behind him, faint in the afternoon heat, he heard the sound of a woman screaming for help and the answering shouts of men as they wakened and went to her rescue.

Gregg frowned. The true story was known only to Pedro and himself. The woman would accuse him of robbery. Pedro, when he had recovered consciousness, would do the same. The saddle of the mount he rode was unmistakable and his very clothing would render him suspicious. No man dressed in worn-out farm clothing would normally be riding a blooded mare with an expensive saddle.

He dug his heels hard against the flanks of the horse, gripped the reins and sent the mount flying out of town.

The quicker he changed horses the better, it was only a matter of time before a posse came riding after him, and in this part of the world horse stealing was the shortest way to earn death at the end of a rope.

Gregg had no desire to be lynched.

2

The stage-coach was a great lumbering construction of wood and leather. The wheels were huge, iron-rimmed and made of stout hickory. Six horses drew the stage over the rutted road, and as Gregg waved, the driver stamped on his brake and hauled at the reins.

'Whoa,' he yelled, then as the stage rocked to a halt stared at Gregg. 'Trouble?'

'Can you sell me a ride?' Gregg stared up at the driver, conscious of the suspicion in the man's eyes. The guard, cradling his shotgun, leaned forward, stared at Gregg, then spat in the dust.

'I guess so.' The driver stared round at the rolling desert. 'Horse give out on you?'

'Rattler got him.' Gregg stooped, lifted his saddle, flung it on top of the coach and jerked open the door. The driver cracked his whip, the stage lurched into motion and Gregg sat down, glad of the rest.

He had walked for almost twenty miles and was beginning to feel it. The livery horse he had brought from a stable had died two days ago and he had had to make it on foot across the rough terrain to the stage route. He still felt uneasy, even though he had left the stolen horse at the livery stable, yet Pedro would still be after him for the money.

He sat and stared out of the window at the rocky, bare, harsh desert through which they were travelling. A man, a business man by the broad-cloth he wore, nodded towards it.

'Bad country.'

'It could be worse.' Gregg didn't want to make conversation. The man sensed it, for pointedly he turned to the other occupant of the coach, an elderly minister, and began to argue on the relative merits of California and Florida. Gregg wasn't interested.

Despite the swaying of the coach he dropped into a light slumber, waking only at the post-stations, where the horses were changed and the chance of a quick meal offered. After three such stages the stage rolled into a small township and the driver yelled that it was the end of the journey. Gregg climbed stiffly from the coach, paid the driver, hefted his saddle and looked for the livery stable.

Johnstown was one of the frontier towns springing up all over the West. It was a depot, a stage halt, a provision store for the miners, Indian fighters, prospectors and ranchers who were beginning to turn a wilderness into a civilized community. The livery stable consisted of a fenced corral, a few barns holding feed and tackle, some stables and a smithy. An old man looked up from where he was shaping a horseshoe as Gregg entered the stables. He put down his hammer, wiped his hands on his apron and waited for Gregg to speak.

'I want a good horse,' said Gregg. 'A good one. Have you anything for sale?'

'Got a stallion,' said the old man, He wiped his mouth with the back of his hand. 'Name's Zeke, run this place with my two boys.'

'Gregg Halmar,' said Gregg. 'What else?'

'A gelding. A good animal. I got it from a man heading west. It went lame on him and he had to leave it. It's all right now though.'

'Let's look at them,' said Gregg.

The old man led the way into the stables and showed Gregg the two horses. Gregg examined them, running his hands down their legs, probing at the fetlocks, looking at their teeth. The gelding quivered a little as he touched the right leg.

'Still sore,' said Gregg. He looked at the stallion. 'This one's no good either. Been ridden too hard and has lost its wind. You got anything else?'

'Maybe.' Zeke found a pipe, stuck it in his mouth, lit it and breathed smoke.

'Got a good mare. Price is two hundred dollars.'

'Show me.'

Zeke didn't move. 'You got two hundred dollars?'

'I'm not wasting your time if that's what you mean.' Gregg stared at the old man, and after a moment Zeke grunted and led the way into the stables. He paused by a stall. 'Here she is.'

Gregg stared at it, entered the stall, examined the horse. When he came out his mouth was a thin slit and his eyes were gleaming.

'You trying to be smart?' He glared at the old man. 'That horse is with foal.'

'Two for the price of one,' said Zeke.

'I want an animal that isn't going to die or lie down on me,' snapped Gregg. 'What's the idea of showing me a mare with foal?'

'Just right for a farm,' said the old man. He squinted at the big man. 'For a farmer you sure act peculiar. What's wrong with them horses I showed you?'

'Nothing — for a farm.' Gregg

realized the old man's perfectly natural mistake. 'Forget the farm, these clothes don't mean nothing. Show me a cowpuncher's horse.'

'That's different.' Zeke took his pipe from his mouth and spat in the dust. 'Why didn't you tell me that you wanted a riding horse?'

'Should I have done?'

'Saved time. I get all sorts come in here. Farmers are the worst. They want something cheap and good, and you just can't get that. Anyways, what's a farmer want with a good working horse? He'd only spoil it.' Zeke led the way into another building. 'These are ranch horses, have a good look at them. When you've decided we can talk about the price. I've got work to do.'

Alone, Gregg examined the horses with careful eyes and probing fingers. He finally selected a deep-chested bay, a gelding with the unmistakable signs of a blooded animal apparent in his lines and the shape of his head.

He led him outside, hitched him to a rail, lifted the hooves and examined the shoes. They were worn and needed replacement.

'How much for this animal?'

'That one?' Zeke quenched the shoe in a tub of water, put it down on the anvil and came towards where Gregg was standing. 'That's old Colonel Price's horse. He lost his hair a month ago, was out in the hills when the Indians jumped him, and I bought it at the auction. A fine horse.'

'How much?'

'Say five hundred dollars.'

'Say three hundred,' snapped Gregg. 'Is it a deal?'

'That horse is worth every cent of four hundred,' said Zeke. 'That's my bottom price and I ain't arguing.'

'It's a deal,' said Gregg. 'But only if you throw in a set of shoes.' He took the money from his pocket, riffled the bills, counted out four hundred dollars. 'Is it a deal?'

'Take me a while to shoe the horse,'

said Zeke, his eyes greedy as he saw the money. 'But if you can wait then it's a deal.'

'I can wait.' Gregg handed the man the money. 'I've got some shopping to do, take me a couple of hours. Long enough?'

'Sure.'

'I'll leave my saddle. Do a good job,' said Gregg.

'I always do a good job,' snapped the old man. He thrust the money into his pocket and took out a printed form. 'I'll give you a bill of sale.' He scrawled with a pencil and passed the paper to Gregg. 'See you later, then.'

The bill of sale the old man had given him made the transaction legal and would be proof of his ownership if ever he were questioned as to the horse. With such a bill he could also sell the mount. Unless a man had such a document he ran the risk of being accused of being a horse thief. Such an accusation wouldn't be made unless the man was a stranger, but all travellers, for their own protection, liked to carry proof of ownership of the mount they were riding.

Gregg next called at the outfitter's. It was a dim, dingy place selling bolts of home-spun flannel shirts, boots, calico and cotton. The owner, a wispy Levantine, rubbed his hands as Gregg gave his orders, and within a short space of time the big man had changed his clothing for the trousers, high boots, shirt and jacket of a cowpuncher. He bought a couple of spare shirts, leather chaps, a wide-brimmed Stetson and a dark bandanna for his neck.

At the gunsmith's he took care over the selection of his weapons.

'I want a rifle,' he told the clerk. 'A Winchester repeater. Got any?'

'Got a good Spencer carbine going cheap,' said the man. 'Or a Henry repeater? Will that do?'

'I prefer a Winchester.'

The man shrugged and lifted one down from the rack on the wall. Gregg tested it, operating the lever and throwing it to his shoulder. It was a good gun, brand new, and he set it to one side.

'You'll take it?'

'Yes.'

'Ammunition too?'

'Naturally.' Gregg watched as the man placed a box of shells on the counter. 'I'll want a scabbard too, a used one if you have it, and a pair of Colts and holsters.'

'New holsters?'

'No.'

The clerk nodded understandingly and reached for weapons and holsters. He knew, as well as Gregg, that most men preferred used holsters to new. The pistols were less inclined to stick, the leather was smoother, the holsters needed no breaking in.

'Let me see those guns.' Gregg held out his hand as the clerk placed a holstered pair of Colts on the counter.

'They aren't new,' warned the clerk. 'A gunslinger carried them until he got himself shot by the sheriff.'

Gregg nodded, examining the weapons. They were standard Frontier Model Colt .45s, single action and each with a barrel seven and a half inches long, the total length of the guns being almost fourteen inches. He opened the side gate, spun the chambers, looked down the barrels. He cocked them, testing the hair-triggers.

'The dogs have been filed,' said the clerk. 'Foresights too. I guess that gunslinger must have fancied himself.' He spoke with the expert knowledge of a man who knew his wares and their uses. Filing of the trigger dogs was common practice among gunfighters who preferred hair-trigger action. Some of them went as far as removing the triggers altogether and letting the weight of the hammer fire the cartridge.

Gregg poised the guns in his hands, balancing them and getting the feel. He crouched, let his right thumb roll back the hammer of the right-hand gun, snapping off five imaginary shots in a smooth blur of motion. As he snapped the hammer for the fifth time he dropped the gun, threw the left-hand one to his right hand and repeated the roll of the hammer. It was the border shift, the trick of a gun-fighter who had learned the habit of changing guns so as not to favour one shooting hand. Gregg repeated the manoeuvre, with his left hand doing the firing, then, with the clerk watching, fired the two guns in unison, left, right, left, right, the clicking of the hammers sounding like a continuous snapping noise.

'Man, but you can use those guns!' The clerk blinked and reached for the holsters. 'I guess you'll take them?'

'I'll take them.' Gregg held them to the light, examining the firing pins. They were unworn.

'I changed them when I got the guns,' said the clerk. 'Most men like new pins in their Colts.' He looked curiously at Gregg. 'You a gunfighter?'

'I can use guns,' said Gregg. He opened the guns, reached for ammunition and loaded each weapon with five cartridges. The empty chamber he placed under the hammer. Colts had no safety catches, and a wise man always took the precaution of leaving an empty chamber under the hammer. The action of cocking the gun, drawing back the hammer, would revolve the chamber and so bring a cartridge into action.

The loading finished, Gregg filled the loops of the cartridge belts, strapped them around his lean waist, slipped the twin guns into the holsters and adjusted them to his liking. He took out money and paid the clerk.

'You want anything else? Shotgun? Bowie?' The man was eager to please.

'A bowie.' Gregg examined the blade, hung the sheath on his belt, slipped the knife into its casing.

'Nothing else?'

'No.'

It was afternoon when Gregg stepped from the gunsmith's. He stood taller, broader, felt more like himself as he strode down the broadwalk, the high heels of his riding boots rapping on the planking, his spurs jingling and the comforting weight of his guns against his thighs. Zeke had shod the horse by the time he returned to the livery stable, and at first the old man didn't recognize the tall, lean cowpuncher as the man who had bought the horse.

'You look different,' he said, stepping back and surveying Gregg from head to foot. 'Now I know why you want a good horse.'

'Why?'

'A man needs a good mount to ride the trails.'

'So he does.' Gregg flung his saddle over the horse, tightened the cinches, adjusted the rifle in its scabbard and looked at the old man. 'Saddle-bags,' he said. 'Got any?'

'Sure.'

'Get them.'

Zeke shuffled off to return with the saddle-bags. Gregg took them, nodded to the old man, put one foot in the stirrups and mounted. Touching the horse with the heels he guided it from the stable and into the town. A store sold him blankets and a bed-roll, together with food, tobacco and a pair of field-glasses.

Towards evening Gregg rode out of town on the trail east.

He rode easily, his firm-muscled body upright in the saddle, his cold blue eyes flickering from side to side as he rode. He did not push his new horse, letting it find its own speed, knowing that he had chosen a good mount. Behind him the miles fell away, the long, winding trail devoid of all other life.

It grew darker, the setting sun throwing his shadow before him. From the distance a coyote howled, another answering it, and for a few minutes the evening was filled with the mournful sound of their cries. A rabbit, suddenly bolting across the trail, caused the horse to snort and jerk at the reins. Gregg soothed it, knowing the high-spirited horse would take a little while to become accustomed to its new owner.

When it was almost dark Gregg halted, riding off the trail into a tiny hollow ringed with scrub. He dismounted, unsaddled the horse, rubbed it down and tethered it. He built a small fire, set a pot of water to boil and undid his blankets. From the saddle-bags he took bacon and flour, cut thick slices from the bacon and, dipping them in the flour set them to cook. With a little water he made a dough, rolled the dough into small balls and dropped them into the hot embers of the fire. The water boiled and he removed the pot, threw in a handful of ground coffee, stirred it, added syrup and stirred again.

Putting aside the coffee he took the bacon, raked the johnny cakes from the embers, broke them open, speared a portion of bacon on the tip of his knife and settled to the business of eating.

He had only just finished when he heard a sound.

It was a peculiar sound, a grunting, cursing, hopeless kind of noise and it came beyond the edge of the firelight. Gregg rose, his right hand dropping to the Colt, his left picking a brand from the fire. He stepped forward, his muscles tensed for action, then as the light from his brand fell on the source of the noise he advanced further.

A man stared up at him.

He was middle-aged, bearded, his face grimed and streaked with sweat. His clothing was torn and stained with dirt. His hands bruised and bleeding, his eyes glazed with shock and fear.

'Help,' he said. 'Help.'

'Easy.' Gregg stopped, lifted the man, carried him back to the fire. 'What's wrong?'

'Rattler.' The man gestured to his left leg. 'Was out riding, trying to cross country and save time. Rattler scared my horse and threw me. Near knocked me out, I guess, because the sidewinder had me before I knew it. Smashed in his head and tried to clean the wound. Then kept walking and hoped I'd hit town.'

'Relax.' Gregg fumbled in his saddle-bags and found a bottle of whiskey. He passed it to the man.

'Take a drink, a small one, then I'll look at your leg.'

'Name's Wilson,' gasped the man. 'Mike Wilson.' Breath hissed between his teeth as Gregg moved his injured leg. 'Hell! That hurts!'

'Relax.' Gregg took his bowie and cut away the cloth. He stared at the wound, inflamed, swollen, crusted with dried blood and dirt. 'You try to tend this?'

'Yes. I cut and bled it hoping to wash out the poison.'

'When did it happen?'

'Two, three days ago. Why?'

'It's turning bad. You won't die of rattler poison, not now, but you may of infection.' Greg took a drink of whiskey and handed the bottle to the sick man. He took his bowie and rested it in the embers of the fire. From his belt he took a cartridge, twisted out the bullet with his teeth and set the case

42

containing the powder down near the injured leg.

'What you aim to do?'

'Some doctoring.' Gregg look at the strained face of the sick man. 'You can take a choice. You can leave it and I'll take you into town tomorrow, or you can trust me.'

'How long to town?'

'Day's ride.'

'Can it last?'

'Maybe.' Gregg picked up his bowie, looked at it, returned it to the fire. 'Maybe not. You might lose the leg and save your life. You might lose both.'

'Hell!' Mike took another drink of whiskey. 'I don't aim to lose no leg. You seem to know what you're doing, stranger, maybe you'd better get on with it.'

'Name's Gregg Halmar,' said Gregg. 'That leg's got infected. I'll have to cut it open, let the poison out, then cauterize it. It'll hurt some, but it'll soon be over. You want me to do it?'

'It hurts like hell as it is,' said Mike.

He gritted his teeth. 'I can't afford to take no chances on losing that leg or being laid up for long. I've got business to attend to. Get cutting.'

'Take a drink.' Gregg passed him the bottle. 'Then find something to bite on, a belt will do. Try not to move. Yell if you want to, but don't move.'

He waited until the man had taken a gulp of whiskey, then took the bottle. He lifted the bowie from the fire, the blade a dull red, and tipped whiskey over it. The hot metal hissed as the spirit hit and cooled it, then holding the sterilized blade Gregg deliberately cut at the festering wound. He cut quickly, cleanly, driving the blade deep and slashing across the swollen, inflamed flesh. Beneath him Mike jerked, groaned, scrabbled at the ground. Blood gushed from the wound, bright red blood mixed with an oozing stream of pus. Dropping the knife Gregg pressed with the balls of his thumbs around the cuts forcing the wound to bleed even more, the rush of blood washing away the infection.

He sat back, his eyes sombre as he stared at the blood.

'You all right, Mike?'

'I guess so.' The man's voice was weak, but he managed to grin. 'Got any more of that firewater.'

'Sure.' Gregg passed the bottle.

'Finished?'

'Almost. You can rest easy and forget about it.' Gregg rose, poured the coffee into a tin cup, rinsed out the pot, filled it with water from his canteen. He set it to boil, ripped his spare shirt into rough bandages, then dropped the strips into the warming water. He took one, wrung it out and wiped the wound.

Blood came as he finished wiping, and Mike groaned at the touch of the cloth. Gregg wiped again, then with one swift motion took the cartridge case, tipped the black powder into the open wound and touched it off with a splinter from the fire. There was a puff of flame, a cloud of smoke, and the powder burned itself out, leaving a cauterized wound. Quickly, before the blood could break through the thin crust, Gregg bandaged it, wrapping the hot strips of cloth around the sore and injured leg.

'That's it.' He rose, tipped away the water and refilled the pot. 'We'll have some coffee now and eat.'

'Yes.' said Mike faintly. 'Eat.'

'You all right?' Gregg stared down at the man. He lifted the limp body and put the whiskey bottle to the flaccid lips. 'Snap out of it, Mike. It's all over, finished. Take a drink and forget it.'

'Thanks.' Mike gulped at the raw spirit, and colour returned to his cheeks. 'Hell, for a doctor you sure are rough.'

'You want to live, don't you?' Gregg took the bottle, stared at the contents, put it in the saddlebag. 'That's enough for now. More whiskey will do you more harm than good. What you need is hot coffee, hot food and warm blankets. Two, three days and you'll be fit to travel.'

'I hope so.' Mike stared down at his bandaged leg. 'I'm late as it is.' He looked at the big man, his hard face limned by the firelight into planes and angles of granite. 'Where did you learn your doctoring?'

'During the war.'

'You North or South?'

'Does it matter?'

'No.' Mike thought about it. 'No, I guess not. Sorry I asked.'

'South,' said Gregg. 'I was captain. I did some doctoring in the hospital they sent me to.' He prodded at the fire. 'I don't want to talk about it.'

'You must have had a rough time.'

'I said that I didn't want to talk about it.'

'Sorry.' Mike stared at the fire. 'I'm a Texan myself, a rancher. Own a few thousand head of prime cattle down Houston way. You ever been down there?'

'No.'

'It's a fine country. The grass is thick and green, the air clear, the prairie rolls

47

for miles as far as you can see. A fine country.'

'So I've heard.' Gregg handed Mike a slice of bacon and a johnny cake. 'What brought you up this way?'

'Looking for something.' The rancher took the bacon and bit into it with the hunger of a man who has been too near the edge of starvation. 'Where are you heading, Gregg?'

'Texas.'

'You are?' Mike paused in his eating. 'Say, that's wonderful!'

'It is?'

'Sure it is, we can ride together.' Mike looked uncomfortable. 'Sorry, guess I'm not able to keep my big mouth shut. Maybe you don't aim to have company.'

'I've no objections,' said Gregg. He turned, the firelight gleaming from his eyes. 'Tomorrow we'll ride on, my horse can take double. I'll get you a horse as soon as I can. You aren't fit to ride alone, not with that leg. Maybe you should rest up somewhere until it's better?'

'I want to get home.' Mike hesitated. 'Look, Gregg, I don't know how to put this, but if you help me now you won't regret it.'

'Are you offering me money?' Gregg stared at Mike, his eyes hard. Mike shook his head.

'Don't get me wrong, Gregg. I don't mean no harm. Back home I've a dozen cowhands on the pay-roll. I figured that if you're heading down my way I could sign you on as from last month. You can quit any time you want to.' He hesitated. 'That is if you want a job; do you?'

'No.'

'How about temporary?'

'Why not?' Gregg smiled. 'All right, I'm working for you until we reach Houston. It looks as if I'm stuck with you, anyway. But I don't want your money.'

'What do you want, then, Gregg?'

'Information and help. Lots of both.'

'Fair enough, what do you want to know?'

'I'll tell you later,' said Gregg. 'Maybe tomorrow, maybe when we reach Houston.' He reached forward and threw dirt over the fire. Better get some rest now.'

Mike nodded and wrapped Gregg's blankets around him. His leg hurt and sleep was shallow. Twice he woke and each time he saw the silent figure of the big man sitting by the fire.

The third time he woke it was dawn.

3

It took three weeks to reach Houston. Texas. Three long weeks during which Mike's leg healed and he managed to rest in the saddle of the horse Gregg had purchased at a livery stable. It wasn't a good horse, but Mike wasn't worried. He had plenty of his own waiting for him when he arrived home.

Gregg, as he rode, was all attention. He stared at the rolling prairie, the great unfenced range which stretched for miles as far as the eyes could see. Great herds roamed those grasslands, the famous longhorn cattle reared by the Texans for the beef markets to the north and east. Cowboys rode guard on the herds, not many, and what few there were were careless and indifferent to strangers. Mike explained why as they rode down the trail.

'Beef just ain't worth stealing, Gregg.

For five dollars each a man can buy as many head as he can use. For six dollars he can pick his cattle and have them delivered anywhere in the State.' The rancher sounded disgusted, and Gregg could guess why. During the war the herds had increased beyond all bounds, for with transportation impossible, Texas at war with the very states which were the best customers, there had been nothing to stop the tremendous increase. Now the state was loaded with cattle no one wanted. No one in the state, that was, though north and east the markets were starved for beef.

The trouble was getting them there.

Mike lived in a rambling hacienda type ranch-house surrounded by a fence and with a well dug not too far away. Beside the ranch-house stood a smithy and feed store for the horses. The bunk shack stood a little further back next to the cooking quarters. Some men lounged about the bunk-house and several more sat on the corral fence watching a horse wrangler breaking in a new steed. They turned as they saw Mike, stared and within seconds were all around him, yelling and calling a shrill welcome.

'We'd just about given you up, boss,' said a pock-marked redhead. He wore two guns, a fancy vest of leather, trimmed and ornamented with silver, and his eyes held the hardness of a man who has lived all his life on the range.

'I'm all right, Red,' smiled Mike. He turned to Gregg. 'Gregg, meet Red Holton, my ramrod. Gregg found me in trouble,' he explained to the foreman. 'Did some work on me and got me to my feet again. Treat him as a friend.'

'Sure.' Red stared at Gregg, and for a moment the two men weighed each other up. The foreman glanced at Mike. 'Any luck?'

'Tell you in the house.' Mike swung from the saddle, Gregg following his example. 'Have the cook rustle up some grub and get someone to take care of these horses.' He handed Red the reins.

'How are things?'

'As usual.'

'No trouble?'

'A little rustling, but they were Mexicans and we scared them off. A few settlers rode in and tried to break sod down in the water pasture. We took care of them too.' Red grinned. 'Should have heard them squawk. We was right gentle too, just scared them into having better sense.'

'No killing?' Mike stared hard at the foreman. 'You know that I won't tolerate any of that stuff.'

'No killing,' said Red. 'But you're too soft, Mike. Let the sheep-raisers come in and you'll cut your own throat. This is cattle country, we got no time for sheep-herders and sod-breakers.' He sounded grim as he spoke, and Gregg recognized the eternal grouse of the cattleman.

The range was free and, in theory, anyone could settle. In theory, but the ranch owners had their own ideas about that. They wanted to keep the range open so that their vast herds could roam at will over the grass, with free access to water. They fought the sheep-herders and settlers with grim determination. Their arguments, to them, were valid. Sheep ruined the grass and they needed the grass for the cattle. Settlers meant fences and restricted water. The cattlemen wanted neither and there had been ugly incidents of settlers waking to find their homes burning, their stock slaughtered, their menfolk shot.

Who was in the right didn't matter and Gregg didn't let himself worry about it. He held no brief for settlers or sheep-raisers, cattlemen or anyone else, he wanted to make himself enough money so that he could build his shattered life anew.

Mike led the way into the ranch-house, and Red followed. The rancher was a widower and lived with an aged Mexican housekeeper and his only daughter. He introduced Gregg to her, a tall, fair-skinned girl, her face freckled from the Texan sun. Her name was Grace, she had been raised on the ranch, and she stared at Gregg with cool appraisal.

'Dad tells me he's indebted to you,' she said. 'He reckons that you saved his life.'

'He could be right,' said Gregg. It was getting dark, and across the table her face showed as a white blur against the windows. Mike, sitting at the head of the table, chuckled, and Red, who as foreman was permitted to eat with the ranch owner, made a sound somewhere between a snort and a grunt.

'Modest, ain't he?'

'Modesty doesn't enter into it,' said Mike. 'I'd have handed in my chips if I hadn't bumped into Gregg. He took care of me, operated on my leg, gave me his blankets. He saved my life, all right.'

'What else could he have done?' Red reached for his coffee, drank it, leaned back in his chair. He reached into a pocket, produced papers and a sack of tobacco, and with quick skill built himself a cigarette. He lit it, inhaling and blowing smoke through his nostrils.

'Nothing,' said Gregg. 'Let's not talk about it.' He toyed with his coffee. 'Or rather let's talk about the future.' He looked at Mike. 'We made a bargain.'

'And you want it settled? Fair enough.' The rancher made no effort to move. 'Speak your mind, Gregg.'

'Now? In company?'

'I can trust my daughter,' said Mike. 'And Red is closer to me than a son. You can talk.'

'As you wish.' Gregg hesitated. 'You said that you'd give me money. I didn't want that, but now I want something else. Information.' He looked at the rancher. 'I'm green, but I'm trusting you. I want you to tell me of conditions here, how to set about a drive, everything.'

'Why, you writing a book?' Red grunted and took the cigarette from his mouth. 'What you want to know?'

'I told you.'

'Yes, but why?'

'My own reasons.'

'Lay off, Red,' snapped Mike. 'So what if Gregg is a greenhorn, does that tell against him?'

'Wastes time,' said the foreman. He looked at Mike. 'Things have been happening while you was away. A couple of buyers came through offering three dollars a head. I rode them off the ranch.' He grinned as if at a pleasant memory. 'Old Sam sold out last week. Couldn't even pay his boys so he shared the stock between them. He raised what he could, loaded his family into a wagon and headed west to California. Crazy old coot! I'll bet the Indians get his hair before he makes it.'

'Sam gone!' Mike shook his head. 'That's bad. We started together.'

'The boys are getting a little restless,' said Red. 'They figure that they are due some back wages. I've talked to them and they stayed.'

'Good.'

'Not so good,' said Red. 'I told them

that you had gone looking for a buyer. They'll expect you to have settled something.' He drew at his cigarette. 'Did you?'

'No.'

'That's bad.' Red inhaled smoke again. 'You can't expect men to wait forever.'

'Theyll get paid,' said Mike, but he spoke with a flat hopelessness. He looked at Gregg. 'Is this talk strange to you?'

'I can guess what you're driving at,' said Gregg.

'I went to try and raise a loan,' said Mike. 'I've got huge herds of cattle, but no ready money. Few people in Texas have. Unless we can sell our cows we can't get money to buy equipment and pay the riders. I'd hoped to make arrangements to sell a small herd in Colorado. I had no luck and was riding back home when the accident happened.'

'Bad,' said Gregg emotionlessly.

'Fred Sprinkler of the Lazy Y tried to

run five hundred head up North,' said Red. 'He got as far as Kansas, and the jayhawks jumped him. Lost ten men, all his beef and came back with a couple of holes in him.' He screwed up his mouth as though he wanted to spit. 'Damn jayhawks!'

'It doesn't seem right,' said Grace. It was the first time she had spoken since the end of the meal. 'Why can't they let us alone?'

'They claim that we owe them money from the war,' said Red. 'They say that they are collecting transit taxes for every head of cattle crossing the State.' He sounded ugly. 'Sprinkler said that they wanted five dollars a head. He couldn't pay it so they jumped him.'

'Robbery,' said Grace indignantly. 'Sheer robbery.'

'Sure, but that doesn't alter things,' said Red. 'Call them outlaws and brigands and you'd be right. But who's going to stop them?' He looked at Gregg. 'Have you any ideas?'

'I'm no policeman,' said Gregg shortly.

'You're no cattleman either,' said Red. 'What are you, mister?'

'That's my business.' Gregg knew that the foreman had stepped beyond the bounds of the Western code in demanding his business. In the West a man was taken for what he claimed to be and treated as such until he proved otherwise. Curiosity was actively discouraged.

'It could be ours too,' said Red. 'We're getting some peculiar people drifting into Texas nowadays. Gunslingers and men from over the Rio Grande. There's talk of rustling and horse stealing and, with only a few of the boys left on the pay-roll, things are liable to turn ugly.'

'I'm no spy,' said Gregg. 'I'm just a man looking for something.'

'Such as?'

'That's my business.' Gregg stared at Mike. It had grown darker and, before he could speak, the housekeeper entered and lit the candles. The dancing flames threw shadows about the big, roughly-furnished room. In their light Grace looked somehow more feminine, her hair softer, her eyes more appealing. Despite the working clothes she wore, shirt, trousers and high boots, she looked suddenly beautiful. Gregg noticed it, noticed too that Red was attracted to the girl. Mike cleared his throat, rose, left the table and walked towards the fire. A small blaze leaped in the grate, for the nights were chill and the flames gave a sense of comfort and snugness. He sat down, the others joining him.

'I'll come to the point,' said Gregg abruptly. 'I want to buy some cattle.'

If he had thrown a bomb he could not have caused a greater impression. Red stared at him, his face betraying his incredulity. Grace gasped, her eyes brilliant with sudden hope. Mike, the rancher, stared thoughtfully at the big man.

'I'll show my hand,' said Gregg. 'I've heard that cattle are fetching as high as forty dollars in the eastern markets. Am I right?'

'Yes.' Mike didn't shift his gaze.

'From what I've heard and from what you told me it is risking the herd and men's lives to try and break a trail through Kansas. Right?'

'Right again.'

'So I've been doing some thinking. I figure that with all the beef here in Texas there must be markets somewhere else. Wyoming, Montana, Idaho, places like that.' Gregg stared at the rancher. 'I trust you, Mike. I'm a greenhorn when it comes to cattle and I admit it. I'd like to buy some cattle and I'd like to buy them from you. I figure that if you reckon you owe me anything you could square it that way.' He smiled at the rancher's expression. 'By selling me good beef, I mean cattle able to travel and travel hard.'

'I'll sell you beef,' said Mike. 'I'll sell anyone beef, but for you I'll cut out the primest head.' He hesitated. 'Look, Gregg, you know what you're doing?'

'I think so.' Gregg reached into his pocket and produced his money. He counted it. His purchases had left him a bare ten thousand dollars. He held it in his hand.

'I've got ten thousand to play with. You told me that the price was five dollars a head. I figure that I can buy fifteen hundred head and leave enough cash for chuck wagons and horses. I can hire men and pay them off at the end of the drive.' He counted out the money. 'Here,' he handed the greenbacks to the rancher. 'Start cutting out the herd.'

'Money!' said Red. 'Real money!'

'I can't take it,' said Mike. He shook his head. 'Hell, Gregg, you're my friend. I can't let you do it.'

'Why not?'

'Because you'll lose both it and your hide, that's why.'

'I don't think so.' Gregg dropped the bills into the rancher's hand. 'One thing is for sure, you can't sell your cattle sitting here. I aim to take a chance. I think that I can drive them up north into Wyoming and sell them there.' He grinned at the rancher. 'It's money, Mike. Will you sell me cattle or do I go somewhere else?'

'It's crazy,' said Grace. 'Crazy, but wonderful.'

'It's taking a chance,' said Red thoughtfully. He hesitated, looking at the money. 'Take it, Mike. With it you can meet some of the pay-roll and keep the boys happy.'

'Yes,' said Mike. He looked at the money. 'Yes, that's right.'

'Good.' Gregg tucked the rest of the money back into his pockets. 'Now maybe you can help me with the rest of the stuff. I'll need a couple of chuck wagons, a couple of cooks, some riders, spare horses and other gear. We can eat beef while travelling so as to cut down on food. We can hunt and live easy. Can you recommend a couple of dozen riders who would be willing to ride with me? I'll pay them well.'

'How well?'

'I figure that the drive will last, say,

three months. Normal wages would be forty a month and all found. I'll need a couple of dozen men, say, a wage bill close on three thousand dollars.' Gregg frowned. 'Say we arrive with a thousand head at forty dollars a head. Normal wages would be about a hundred and twenty dollars a man. Say we work on a bonus system based on a thousand head.' He looked at Mike. 'I'll pay a flat rate of five dollars a head sold, to be split equally among the riders. Fair enough?'

'Double wages, maybe more, maybe less.' Mike nodded. 'Sounds fair.'

'Sounds good,' said Red. 'I wouldn't mind joining in on that.'

'You can't,' said Grace. 'You're needed here.'

'I'm getting tired of riding herd,' said Red. 'I want action. I want to get on the move and see things roll.' He grinned. 'It sounds good to me.'

'Yes,' said Mike thoughtfully. He looked at Gregg. 'Do you know the country up that way?'

'Some. I used to prospect in that region before the war. Did some hunting and panning for paydirt 'way back when the Indians were on the loose all over that section.'

'Do you know a trail?'

'No, but I can find one.' Gregg shrugged. 'All right, so I'm taking a chance, but I think that it's worth it. Anyway, it's my neck and my money. If I can reach a good market then I'll make myself a pile of cash. I'm willing to take the chance.'

'I — ' said Mike, then paused. Grace smiled at him.

'Go on, Dad, say it. I know what's in your mind.'

'Partners,' said Mike. He looked at Gregg. 'That is if you're willing.'

'I don't get it.' Gregg frowned. 'What are you driving at?'

'I'd like to come with you,' said the rancher. 'Look, I've got the men, the chuck wagons, the horses. I've got more cattle than I know what to do with and I know how to drive them. If you know the country and are willing to put in your money we can make a joint effort.'

'Keep talking,' said Gregg. He was interested. The rancher obviously knew far more about the handling of cattle than he did.

'You say you had ten thousand dollars. All right. Chip it all in. In return I'll provide everything we need. We'll run a bigger herd, say five thousand head, and we'll split even after the men have been paid. Suit you?'

'Wait a minute,' protested Gregg. 'My money will only buy two thousand head. Why should you put in more than me?'

'I can sell myself my own cattle at four dollars a head,' said Mike. He shrugged. 'I'm not being generous, you could buy for that price yourself with the ready money you have. If you didn't worry too much about brands you could have them for less. There are too many men handy with a running-iron who would like to pick up some ready money.' He looked at Gregg. 'Is it a deal?'

'I don't know,' said Gregg slowly. 'I figured on being the boss of my own outfit. Maybe you won't agree with the way I want to go and the way I want to do things. Once we start there'll be no time, for fighting among ourselves. It'll be hard going all the way.

'Mike's had trail experience,' said Red. 'Have you?'

'No.'

'Then that makes him the boss, doesn't it?'

'Not from where I'm standing,' said Gregg. 'I'm thinking of the future. What happens if I want to go one way and Mike the other? The men will follow him and I'll be left stranded.' He shook his head. 'That's a risk I don't intend to take.'

'We can solve that,' said Mike. 'I'll be in charge of the herd while you be in charge of the trail we take. Fair enough?'

'Split authority is worse than no

authority at all,' said Gregg. 'When I give an order I want it to be obeyed, immediately and without argument.'

'That's the officer speaking,' said Grace. 'You were an officer, weren't you?'

'Captain,' said Gregg shortly. 'Confederate Army.'

'I thought so.' Grace looked pleased with herself for having guessed. 'What brought you so far from home?'

'How do you know that my home isn't in these parts?'

'The way you talk, the way you act, a dozen little things. You seem to be more of a gentleman than the usual saddle-drifters we get around here. And yet you say you prospected the country. I don't get it.'

'You're curious about me,' said Gregg. 'All right, as we may do business together, you have a right to know. My uncle used to live in Colorado. He staked a claim and I lived with him for a spell. The war came and I went back home to enlist. My parents owned a plantation and my two brothers were already in the militia. They were both killed in an Indian raid a couple of years ago. I managed to live through it, but when I went back home my people were dead and the house had been burned. So I came West.'

'Why?'

'I wanted to find a man,' said Gregg shortly. 'I found him, let's leave it at that.'

There was something in his voice which warned the girl that he meant what he said. She shrugged, smiled, and looked at her father.

'Well, Dad?'

'I don't know,' said the rancher, he wasn't eager to take second in command. 'Just where did you intend heading?'

'Wyoming.' Gregg rose and rested his hand against a map which hung on the wall. It was a crude map, showing nothing but the general nature of the country and splotched with white portions which meant that no one knew just what was there.

'We head north, cross the Red River, cut across Oklahoma, slice Kansas, into Colorado and along the Rockies into Wyoming. If the country is suitable we will be able to swing into Nebraska and South Dakota. There might be a railhead pushed that far west by that time or, as I've heard, we'll find buyers for the cattle among the miners. Those boys work hard and crave fresh meat. They are tired of game and buffalo and want beef. We should get forty dollars a head for them anywhere in that territory.'

'That's over a thousand miles,' said Red. 'A long drive.'

'We can make it. We can hunt and live off the country, eat beef if we have to, and take enough men with us to protect the herd against Indians and jayhawks. We might dodge them if we bear west, no need to look for trouble.'

'All right,' said Mike. 'You be the boss. Red will work with you under me. Right, Red?'

'Sure.'

'First thing in the morning go and recruit some men. Pick tough *hombres*, fully armed and with good mounts. You can take horses from the corral. We'll take spare horses, two to a man, and a couple of chuck wagons. When you've got the men we can start the round up. With any sort of luck we can be on the trail within a week.' He rose. 'That's settled.'

'Almost,' sad Grace. She lifted the coffee pot, poured the cups full, passed them around. 'A toast! To success!'

They drank.

4

Five thousand head of longhorn cattle moved slowly towards the Red River. Riders flanked them, hard-faced cowboys dressed in thick trousers and flannel shirts. Leather jackets and chaps, Stetsons and bandannas. Each man was armed, some with one pistol, mostly with two, each man having a rifle and plenty of ammunition. They rode their horses as if born in the saddle, and their calls echoed above the lowing of the masses of steers.

It was a stirring sight, and Gregg, sitting on his horse ahead and to one side of the cattle drive, felt his hopes rise as he looked at the smooth way the riders handled the cattle. Beside him, Red, his sunburned face split into a wide grin, rolled a cigarette.

'It's good to see,' said the foreman with deep feeling. 'There's nothing like a round-up and cattle drive to take a man's mind from his troubles.'

Gregg nodded, not speaking, his eyes narrowed as he stared through the dust. Mike came riding towards him, Grace at his side. They halted, turning their horses to watch the cattle.

'Well, here we go,' said Mike. 'We've been travelling for a week now and have made good time. This is where you leave us, Grace.'

'I know.' She didn't argue, all that was over. At first she had wanted to come with them, but Gregg and Mike had been against it. Both, but for different reasons, did not want her along. Mike because he knew the way would be rough and full of peril, Gregg because he feared the impact a lone woman would have on the rough cowboys after long weeks away from civilisation. Grace had listened to them, agreed to remain behind, and would wait at the ranch for their return.

She looked at Gregg and put out her hand, slender and firm in its glove.

'Take care and watch yourself. You too, Red.' She shook hands, kissed her father and then, without a backward glance, was riding back down the way they had come. Texan women, like Texan men, could be as hard as iron when the necessity arose.

'We're making good time,' said Mike as the two chuck wagons came abreast. 'Fifteen miles a day, sometimes more. We should reach the river in a few days.'

'We'll swing to the west at Fort Worth,' said Gregg. He studied a map before him. 'You know this country so there's no need for me to break trail. We'll ford the river at the shallows and press on into Oklahoma. From then on we'll have to watch our step.' He stared at the cowboys riding at the fringes of the herd.

'They're good boys,' said Red. 'I picked them myself. Some of them might be a trifle rough, but what do you expect?' He smiled. 'I guess you can handle them.'

'I will if I have to.' Gregg stared at a squat man riding past 'Who is that?'

'Curly Watson. They call him Curly on account of he's got no hair. Was knocked out during an Indian raid and woke to find himself scalped. A doctor sewed him up. They say he wears his hat all the time, even to sleep in.'

Gregg turned his head and stared after the cattle.

'I'll ride ahead for a spell and look for a camp. Come with me, Red?'

'Why not.' The foreman winked at Mike. 'Why do you want me?'

'Tell you when we're riding.' Gregg nodded to Mike, spurred his horse, and rode after the herd. They soon passed it and headed into the country beyond. Red knew the terrain, and as they loped forward the cloud of dust behind them shrank and vanished in the distance.

'How far do you reckon the herd can travel before bedding down?' asked Gregg after a while. Red turned, stared about him and shrugged.

'A fair piece. You never driven cattle

77

before, have you, Gregg?'

'No.'

'Well, there are certain things you'll have to remember. At the moment the cows are fit and can cover this type of ground without too much trouble. I guess that we can manage twenty miles a day, that's pushing them, but they can stand it. Later on, when they're getting thin, we'll have to slow down, fifteen, maybe twelve miles a day. Then when we near the selling place we'll rest them up for a few days, let them put on some fat.' He chuckled. 'Makes them look good to the buyers.'

'They'll look good no matter what condition they arrive in,' said Gregg. 'At the moment speed is important. The less time we spend on the trail now the more time we'll have later on.'

'Why?' Red was interested. 'What's the hurry?'

'Winter is only a few months off,' said Gregg. 'It won't matter here, but further north we'll get snow and ice. I don't want to find myself snow-bound with five thousand head of cattle. We've got to push on and beat the weather.'

'We'll beat it,' said Red. He looked about him and smelt the air. Guess we can camp here. There's water and good grass.'

'Couldn't we push on a piece?'

'Sure, but then we'll have to tire them out. The next good place is ten miles further on.' Red chuckled again. 'Don't worry, Gregg, we're all as eager as you are to get rid of the herd. The sooner we can turn this beef into hard money the better we'll like it. Your worries will come later. Five thousand steers aren't something you can hide or move very easily. And we've got a long way to go.'

He was right.

Gregg thought about it as he sat before the fire that night. From where he sat he could see the dim bulk of the cattle as they cropped the grass and settled themselves for sleep. On the still air, thin and plaintive, came the sounds of the guarding riders, singing as they steered their mounts around the huddled beasts. They sang, not only to keep themselves company, but to soothe the herd. Red dipped his pannikin in the water bucket, filled it from the coffee pot and sat beside Gregg.

'Makes you feel good to hear them,' he said. 'Sometimes I feel like taking a gun and shooting some of them, but on the whole it makes you feel good.' He sipped at his coffee. 'What did you think of Grace?'

'What?'

'You heard me. Grace, Mike's daughter. What did you think of her?'

'A fine girl. Why?'

'I aim to marry her,' said Red. 'That's all.'

'Nice,' said Gregg. He knew what the other was getting at. He was a stranger with all a stranger's glamour, while Red was the boy who had grown up with her. The foreman was, not unnaturally, jealous of the impression Gregg had made.

'I think so,' said Red. His voice

deepened, became harsh. 'I ain't much good at fancy talk, but the way I feel about her can't be put into words. I'd take a gun to any man who tried to take her away from me.'

'Why?'

'Because she's my girl,' said Red. 'That's why.'

'Killing won't make her yours if she doesn't figure it that way,' said Gregg. 'You can't win a woman's heart by force.'

'I'd still shoot any man who came between us.'

'Are you thinking of me?'

'Did I say so?'

'No.' Gregg stared at the foreman. 'Don't get me wrong, Red. Grace means nothing to me. But if she did you wouldn't stop me from trying to win her. Threats wouldn't stop me and they never have. If you've got a grief bring it out and let's have a look at it. If it's gunplay you want, then you can have that too. But not now. Not until we've delivered and sold the cattle.'

'You a gunfighter, Gregg?'

'I can handle a gun.'

'Maybe.' Red stared into the fire. 'Forget it. I guess that I'm like a new-broke colt, scared of my own shadow. Time for talk is when talk's needed. Time for gunplay is after the talking's done.'

'Rest easy,' said Gregg. He smiled at the foreman. 'Let's join the others.'

'And Grace?'

'You told me. She's your girl.' Gregg slapped the other man on the shoulder. 'Better take my advice, Red. Rope and brand her as soon as you can. From what I saw of her she's a woman with a mind of her own. Maybe she'll get impatient waiting for you to make up your mind to ask the question.'

'I'll ask her as soon as we get back.'

'And if she says no?'

'I'll take it.' Red grinned, threw away the dregs of his coffee and rose to his feet. 'Some of the boys have a poker game going. Let's sit in.'

The game was held on a spread

blanket illuminated by a lantern hung from one of the chuck wagons. The cooks, their duty done, leaned against the high-wheeled wagons or tended to their chores. One of them wiped his hands on his apron and came limping towards Gregg. He dropped his voice.

'Say, Gregg, one of those *hombres* is a sharper. Better watch him.'

'Which one?'

'A man called Jud. A big man with a couple of guns. He's got a friend with him, a greaser.'

Gregg nodded and moved into the circle of lamplight. Jud, big, swarthy, his mouth almost hidden beneath a sweeping moustache, looked up then concentrated on his cards. His companion, a little Mexican, was busy as he dealt. His nimble fingers flickered the pasteboards as he passed them to the other players.

Some of the men, recognizing Gregg, made room for him to sit in the game. He did so, hunkering down and waiting for the next pot. He threw money into the ante, picked up his cards, bid, raised, threw in his hand. The play meant nothing to him, he was too aware of the dangers of a card-sharp among his crew.

Gregg was no moralist and knew that it took all kinds to make a world, but he had no time for cheating gamblers. Not because of the methods they used, but because of the effects they produced. They had a long, hard trail before them and he had no intention of letting this pair rook the others of their money and then ride off into the night. They weren't true cowboys, they were criminals after what they could get.

And he had no time for men who hoped to gain at his expense.

The play lasted for another hour before he was certain that the cook had been correct in his suspicions. The big man and the greaser were operating the oldest system known to poker. They were pushing up the betting until the others were squeezed out and then one would yield the pot to the other. It wasn't clever, but it was effective. It was only a matter of time before they won the clothes, guns, saddles and equipment of the others.

Unless they got themselves lynched first.

'Bet five dollars,' said Jud, squinting at his cards.

'Raise five,' said the greaser.

'I'll stay,' said Curly. He reached into his pockets, found the money and added it to the pot. Two others stayed and Gregg looked thoughtfully at the pot.

'Raise ten more,' he said.

Jud grunted and stayed, as did his friend. Curly swore, but remained in the game. The others threw in their hands.

'Discards.' The greaser held the pack. Jud took two cards, Curly one, Gregg two and the greaser gave himself one. The betting commenced.

Gregg knew that, according to the draw, Curly and the greaser either had tried to fill a straight or a flush, had two pairs, or held three of a kind. No man in his right mind would try to fill an inside straight and the odds were against both of them having filled a flush. Knowing Curly's play, Gregg knew that the man had either filled his flush or held a full house. The greaser could have held anything. Jud himself probably had the same hand as Gregg had drawn, three of a kind. Gregg had not improved his hand. From his expression neither had Jud. The fact did not stop him betting.

'Ten dollars.'

'Raise ten,' said Curly.

'And ten again,' said Gregg.

'Kid's play,' said the greaser. 'I'll raise twenty.'

'And twenty,' grinned Jud. He didn't care how high he raised the stakes. High enough would squeeze the others out and leave the pot between him and the greaser. No matter who won they would share it afterwards.

'Hell!' said Curly. 'I'm running out of money. Stake my rifle for a hundred dollars.'

The others nodded, a good rifle was worth more than that. Gregg stared at the heap of coins in front of the players.

'How much money you got?' he asked. According to the rules of the game, they were playing table stakes, the players had to answer.

'Hundred and fifty dollars,' snarled Jud. He had the most. Gregg counted out his money, a hundred and fifty dollars, and threw it in the pot. Now, according to the rules, the others either had to meet the sum or take a part of the pot.

'What's the idea?' snapped Jud.

'Simple.' Gregg rested back until he sat on his heels. 'When I play cards I like to play honest poker. Now drop your cards, get your stuff and get out.'

'What?' Jud tensed, his hand poised over his gun butt. 'You saying I'm cheating?'

Such an accusation was usually the prelude for gunplay. Gregg knew it, everyone knew it. Men recoiled as they expected the blast of guns to echo through the night.

'I told you to get your stuff and leave camp,' said Gregg evenly. 'I don't want you to ride with us. Not you or your friend. Now move before I do something about it!'

'Are you saying I cheated?'

'Yes,' said Gregg, and his hands moved so fast that no one saw what really happened. Guns appeared in his two fists as if by magic, each pointing to one of the two gamblers. Jud, his Colt still in its holster, gulped, and the greaser cried out with fear.

'Get on your feet,' said Gregg. 'Curly, take charge of the money, count it, give each man what he has lost.' He released the hammers of the twin Colts. 'I want no gunplay here,' he said quietly. 'But I'm willing to settle things any way you choose. Well?'

'I'll take you,' said Jud. He was a big man used to dirty fighting.

'Drop your guns.' Gregg waited until the man had unbuckled his gunbelt. He undid his own weapon belts and handed them to the squat man. 'Ready?'

Jud grunted flung himself forward, and his fist, as big and as hard as a boulder, slammed towards Gregg's face. Gregg ducked, sent his own fist smashing against the other man's nose with an impact which sent blood spurting from the broken organ, then followed it with three whip-lash blows to the body. Jud swore, jerked up his knee, then flung himself forward and tripped the big man. As Gregg hit the dirt, he rolled, avoiding the vicious rake of the spur which Jud had aimed at his face, a rake which would have torn and gashed his face to the bone, blinding and scarring him for life.

As quick and as lithe as a cat, Gregg jumped to his feet, avoided a savage kick at his groin, then drove in with fists pounding the big man about the face and neck.

It was dirty fighting, all-in fighting, with each man trying to beat the other into insensibility. Jud used every trick he knew, from trying to hook Gregg's legs with his long spurs, to butting with his head. He gave that up when Gregg sent a smashing blow against his mouth, splitting his lips, and as Jud spat out blood and broken teeth he suddenly reverted to the beast that he was.

He dived towards the fire, snatched up the pot of boiling coffee and flung it with all his force towards where Gregg was standing. Curly yelled as some of the hot liquid seared his hands, and he dropped the guns he was holding. Gregg, leaping sideways, managed to dodge the scalding liquid, but as he jumped he stumbled, and before he could recover himself Jud was on him, kicking and raking with the long, sharp rowels of his spurs.

'Get him, Jud,' screamed the greaser. 'Rip him open.'

A spur dashed towards Gregg's face. He rolled, grabbed at the foot and hung on to the boot. Jud snarled, jumped up in the air and brought his other boot down towards Gregg's face. Had the blow landed, the fight would have been over. Gregg would have been killed beneath the savage fury of the other's attack. He saved himself in the nick of time.

Releasing the hold on the foot, he twisted, dodged the blow and with a sudden explosion of energy rose to his feet. Jud staggered back, his mouth working and his eyes glistening in the firelight. He fumbled with the back of his collar, crouched, then sprang forward.

'Watch it, Gregg!' called Curly. 'He's got a knife.'

Jud had. He had ripped it from the sheath below his collar and now came forward, the razor steel gleaming in the firelight. He thrust, and as Gregg swayed aside changed the direction of the blow to a vicious slash. Fire burned along Gregg's side as the steel slit his skin, then, moving with quick desperation, he had closed it, caught the knife arm and, turning trapped it against his body.

Jud pounded at him, slamming heavy blows against his back and kidneys, but Gregg ignored the blows. He concentrated on the hand holding the knife, twisting the wrist until the fingers slowly, reluctantly, opened and the knife fell free. He stooped, snatched up the blade and, turning with it in his hand, met Jud's charge face to face.

The knife slipped home.

Jud felt it, felt the burning pain as the steel plunged between his ribs, and his face went slack. Gregg felt the jar of impact and knew that, more by accident than design, he had killed the big man. He stared as Jud slowly collapsed, then looked at the blood-stained knife in his hand. It had been an accident, but he didn't worry about that. Jud would have killed him, almost had, and in return he had killed Jud.

He dropped the knife and stared down at the body.

'You killed him!' It was the greaser. He stared at Gregg, his eyes narrowed with hate. 'You killed him, you butchering swine! I'll make you pay for this.'

'I'm ready,' said Gregg evenly. 'Any way you want it.'

He held out his hand, took the guns Curly gave him, strapped them around his waist.

'Jud was a no-good cheating sidewinder,' he said. 'And so are you. If you want to make anything of it, reach for your irons.'

'I'll get you for this,' screamed the greaser. 'I'll see that you get yours. I know what you're doing and where you're going and I've got friends that'll settle you for what you did to Jud. I — ' He broke off, conscious that he had said too much.

'String him up,' growled Curly. 'He's liable to raise the jayhawks against us. Get rid of the scum.'

Other men murmured agreement. A private quarrel was one thing and no one would dream of interfering, but the greaser had made threats against them all, and each man knew just how vulnerable they were. Rustlers, jay-hawks, they could swoop down and kill and be off before the cowboys could defend themselves.

'You heard what they said,' said Gregg. 'You've talked too much. Make your play.'

'No.' The man licked nervous lips. 'You're fast, too fast. It would be murder.'

'I'll give you your chance,' said Gregg. 'This quarrel started between you and me. Let's keep it that way. You can fight me or I'll leave it to the boys to deal with you. The choice is yours.'

'They'll lynch me.' The man was almost livid with fear.

'Then make your play.'

'Wait. What if I win? What then?'

'You take your horse and gear and ride out of camp. No one will touch you.' Gregg didn't have to elaborate. In the West a man's word was his bond. Still the greaser hesitated, even though he knew he had no choice.

'I'll give you a chance,' said Gregg.

'I'll count to three. On the count of one you reach for your gun. On the count of three I'll reach for mine. Satisfied?'

It was fair, nothing could have been more fair, and the cowboys muttered as they heard the proposition. They felt that Gregg was getting himself murdered for no good reason. Gregg moved before they could speak.

'One!'

The greaser gulped and grabbed for his gun. He tried to be in too much of a hurry and, as Gregg had known, he let urgency ruin his co-ordination.

'Two!'

The man snatched at the butt of his gun, drew it, raised his other hand, the left hand, and brought it down towards the hammer.

'Three.'

Gregg drew, thumbed back the hammer, aimed and fired in one swift motion. Even at that he hadn't fired first. The greaser had begun to fan his gun, striking the hammer with the stiffened edge of his left palm. It was a method of gunplay for which any decent gunfighter had nothing but contempt. It was showmanship, but that was all. By fanning a gun a man could fire five shots so fast that the individual explosions blended into one, but that was all. Accuracy, steadiness, the iron fact that in a gunfight only one shot really counted, the one that hit the target, was forgotten.

So Gregg stood, taking his time, while the greaser tried to fire five shots instead of the one which really counted. Lead whined about him as he aimed, but when he pressed the trigger the opposition ceased. The greaser slumped. a neat round hole between his eyes. One shot, aimed and deliberate, had been enough.

'All right,' said Gregg, staring round at the watching cowboys. 'The show's over. If any of you feel that I've been hard now's the time to say so. If any of you feel like quitting, get your gear and get out. But from now on there'll be no more of this sort of thing. Any man who wants to shoot it out with me can take his chance. Fist fights are out.'

He slipped the Colt back into its holster and looked up as Mike came towards him. The rancher's face was dark with anger. He gulped as he saw the two dead men.

'Trouble?'

'Some.' Gregg shrugged as he stared down at the bodies. He had seen too many men die, decent men, to worry about a couple of cheating gamblers. 'It's all over now.'

'You sure?'

'I'm sure.' Gregg stared at the cowboys. 'Hit the sack, boys. We've a hard day's work ahead and you'll need the rest.'

'That's right,' echoed Red. 'You heard what the boss said. Break it up now.'

He shook his head as he stared after Gregg.

5

Red River, and five thousand head of cattle beating the water into a muddy froth, the chuck wagons dragged across by brute force, the horses and riders threshing and adding to the din and noise and apparent confusion. Apparent only because the cattlemen knew what they were doing and had long ago reduced the fording of rivers to a fine art. Then the hills of Oklahoma, the rolling grass, the plentiful water as the herd plodded on its steady way northward.

Day after day they moved towards the north, and night after night they slept beneath the stars while the cowboys rode on their circuits, their eyes watchful for strangers. They were pleasant days and easy nights and the herd made good time. Mike rode at the front with Red the foreman, the chuck wagons rolled at the rear, stopping to prepare food for the cowboys and serve endless coffee. Ahead of them, miles ahead, Gregg and Curly, the man he had chosen to ride with him, scouted and sought out the trail the herd would take.

Then as they neared the Kansas border the threat of the jayhawks became suddenly real.

Curly saw it first, a thin plume of dust in the far distance, and when they reached it they found a buckboard holding a dead woman, a dying man and an adolescent boy. Whiskey revived the man long enough for him to gasp his story.

'We was heading West,' he whispered. 'Me, Maria, Lemmy and some other folk. We had some stock and wagons and was doing fine. Then the jayhawks jumped us. They wanted a thousand dollars to let us through. We had no money so they took our stock. We tried to stop them and they shot us up.' His eyes glazed as he stared towards the boy. 'He's the only one left.'

'We'll take care of him,' promised Gregg. 'How many?'

'Maybe fifty, I wouldn't be sure. There's lots of them all along the border. Outlaws, owlhoots, gunmen and sidewinders. I figure — '

He died before he could say what was on his mind.

With shovels from the buckboard Gregg and Curly dug graves for the couple. Lemmy, the boy, seemed dazed with shock and proved no help. Gregg gave him instructions how to find the herd, told him to ask for food, then sent him on his way. His face as he looked at Curly was grim.

'You any good at scouting, Curly?'

'Try me.' The squat man grinned. 'If you're thinking what I think you're thinking then I'm with you all the way.'

'Those jayhawks have to be wiped out,' said Gregg. 'They aren't anything more than killing outlaws. All their talk of patriotism is just hot air. The only thing they understand is hot lead.' He grew thoughtful.

'Ambush,' said Curly. 'But how?'

'We'll scout. We'll find a place and get some of the boys. Then when the main bunch catch up, the jayhawks will get a reception they didn't expect.' Gregg spurred his horse. 'Come on, Curly, we've got work to do.'

They found the place late in the afternoon. It was a long, shallow valley which would provide a perfect camp site for the cattle. To one end it narrowed before opening out on to the rolling prairie beyond. Gregg stared up at the summit of the ridges to either side, measured them with his eye and shook his head.

'Too far.'

'You think so?' Curly looked doubtful. 'We could set men up on those ridges and they could give us word of anything coming this way.'

'We'll do that and more,' said Gregg. Again he scanned the sides of the valley, estimating with a soldier's eye, range, distance, angles of cross-fire and cover. 'We'll do it this way. We'll place riflemen in the underbrush ready to cut loose at a signal. They can reach here and we'll take back their horses to the herd. It'll mean a long wait, but they must stand it.' He twisted his horse and headed back the way they had come. 'Ride, Curly, we haven't much time.'

Back at camp he told Mike of his plans.

'The valley is directly on the trail,' he said. 'Long before we can get out of their territory the jayhawks will have spotted us and be riding down to make their demands. The trick is for us to make them meet us where we are ready for them.' He made marks in the dust. 'Look. We place men with rifles, food and ammunition on both sides of the valley. They must wait there for perhaps three days, and the waiting won't be easy. They can set guards on the ridges to warn them of the jayhawks.'

He made more marks.

'We come along here. We drive the

cattle and travel fast. If the jayhawks catch up with us before we reach the valley then we'll have to make a running fight for it, but I don't think that will happen. We can send out scouts and we'll know what is happening. I think that we can get the cattle to the valley in good time.'

'And then?'

'Then we shoot them down like the dogs they are.'

'Murder?' Mike looked uncomfortable. 'I don't know as if I like that.'

'Call it war. We'll give them their chance, but if they try anything we mustn't hesitate. Leave the talking to me. Once I give the signal let every man draw and shoot to kill. No fancy stuff, we've got to get them before they get us.'

Gregg stared at Mike and Red. Curly, standing behind the big man, said nothing.

'Anyone got anything to say?'

'I saw that boy,' said Red slowly. 'The one you sent back. He seemed half crazy. I told one of the cooks to take care of him.'

'He saw his Ma and Pa shot down before his eyes,' said Gregg. 'That's the sort of people we're dealing with.' He looked at Curly. 'You know the men better than I do. Find ten of the best rifle shots, get some food and ammunition from the chuck wagons and take them up to the valley. You know what to do.'

'Five a side,' said Curly. 'And bring back their horses. Right?'

'Yes?'

'Tell them this isn't a game. No shouting, no yelling, no shooting in the air. Aim to kill, shoot the horses if they have to, but get those jayhawks.'

'Leave it to me,' grinned the squat man. 'This is going to be fun.'

'Maybe.' Gregg stared at Red and Mike. 'Right. Now we get on the move. I want the cattle to reach the valley as soon as possible. I want to arrive in good daylight. If we have to travel all night then we must do it.'

'It'll wear out the cows,' protested Mike.

'They can eat and rest in the valley.'

'Travelling at night's not the thing,' said the rancher. 'They don't like it.'

'Then they can learn to like it.' Gregg stared at the rancher, his lips a thin line in his sunburned face. 'Listen, Mike, and listen good. This isn't a game we're playing. We're bumping into real trouble, those jayhawks will shoot us and take our cattle unless you pay them. Have you the money to meet their so-called taxes?'

'You know that I haven't.'

'Then leave this to me. I've had experience fighting guerrillas and other bands, and I know what to do. Arguing will get us nowhere. We've got to hit hard, fast, and for keeps. We've got to wipe them out then get moving before others can arrive to pick our bones. From what I hear each band of jayhawks keeps to its own territory. We'll cut a path through them and be deep into Colorado before the rest can get after us.'

'I suppose you know what you're doing,' said Mike slowly. 'Anyway, you're the boss.'

'Yes,' said Gregg. 'I'm the boss.' He rose and stared over the cattle. They had halted for the noon meal. Curly and his picked men had galloped off, the men excited as if they were going to a party. The other cowhands cursed their luck at being left behind. They looked up from the pot of beans and bacon into which they dipped their spoons and loaded their plates.

'Move!' said Gregg. Rapidly he told them what was going to happen. 'Now let's see you cover ground. Hurry!'

They covered twenty miles that day and when the cattle finally settled to rest they were jumpy and tired from exertion. At dawn they were on the move again, paused only for noon eating, and pressed on until after dark. Despite his haste, Gregg admitted that they couldn't travel at night. The terrain was too rough, the beasts too nervous, the danger of a stampede too great. So they rested, and late in the next afternoon a scout reported seeing a distant band of figures.

'Jayhawks?'

'Couldn't tell.' The scout gulped coffee, handed him from the moving chuck wagon and bit at a piece of corn bread. 'They was a long ways off.'

'How many?'

'Ten, maybe a dozen.'

Gregg nodded, his eyes thoughtful. The figures could have been a scouting party or a small band of jayhawks. He stared up at the sun. Allowing for a rest tonight they would reach the valley by mid-morning tomorrow. If the jayhawks held off until then everything would work out right.

They did. They gathered, but did not intercept the herd until they had entered the valley and, wise in the ways of war, Gregg knew why. The jayhawk commander was an intelligent man. He knew that the cattle, bottled in the valley, would have to mass and move slowly through the narrow part to the plains beyond. He knew, too, that the cowboys would be at a disadvantage and if there was any trouble his men would have to drop on the riders. He was intelligent enough to time his attack to his best advantage. He was not intelligent enough to grant others the same foresight.

Gregg was riding point, Mike and Red to the right and left of him, the other cowpunchers strung out in line towards the sides of the valley. Gregg turned and Curly, waiting for the signal, rode alongside.

'Where are the men?'

'In the underbrush to either side just at the narrowest point.' The squat man was excited, eager for action.

'Good.' Gregg stared ahead to where a plume of dust rose towards the clear blue of the sky. 'Halt the cattle. Bring the men to the front and see that every man knows what to do. Move!'

Curly grunted and rode away, shouting orders. The plume of dust ahead came nearer and at the foot and just before it a long line of mounted men became visible as they galloped forward.

The jayhawks!

They rode with a supreme assurance in their own might, rough men, all heavily armed, mostly bearded. Some were veterans of the Civil War, others ex-guerrillas, still others mere adventurers styling themselves as tax-collectors and ruling the Kansas border with the might of their guns. They rode to within a few yards of where Gregg sat his horse, then, drawing rein, stood in a long line and faced the cowpunchers.

'Fifty.' Mike wet his lips. 'Fifty at least.'

'Relax,' said Gregg. He waited for the jayhawks to speak.

'A fine herd,' said a big bearded man. He wore a faded blue uniform, the Captain's insignia tarnished and dirty. 'You the boss?'

'I am.' Gregg let his eyes run down

the line of watching men.

'You're in Kansas territory,' said the leader. 'You know that?'

'No law against it, is there?'

'Not if you get permission to cross.' The leader rose in his saddle, scanned the herd, then sat back again. 'We've had a lot of trouble with you Texans. During the war you caused us a lot of grief. We aim to get even.'

'The war's over,' said Gregg.

'Maybe, but wars have got to be paid for.' The jayhawk was enjoying himself. 'We figure on collecting taxes from everyone crossing into Kansas. Pay up and smile and no harm will come to you.'

'And if we don't?'

'Then you ain't going to get very far.' The leader glanced at his men. 'We don't care either way. Money or cattle, one's as good as another to help repair the damage you Rebels caused during the war.

'How much?' Gregg was getting impatient of this bickering.

'Now you're talking.' The leader ran

his eyes over the herd again. 'I figure that you've got close to six thousand head in that herd.'

'Five thousand.'

'All right, so we'll call it five thousand.' The jayhawk shrugged. 'I ain't a man to argue. Anyways, the tax is a dollar a head. We let the cowboys and their horses through free. Call it a nice round even figure. Five thousand dollars.' He held out his hand. 'Gold or greenbacks, none of your Confederate money.'

'Thanks,' said Gregg. He didn't move. 'If we pay it do we get an escort to the border?'

'Sure.'

'How many men?'

'What's the difference?' The jayhawk was becoming impatient. 'Five thousand dollars in hard money. Pay and get moving.'

'And if we don't?'

'You'll find out.' The leader stiffened. 'You going to pay?'

'Yes,' said Gregg. 'What else can we do?'

His hand dropped as though it were going to his pocket, and then, with baffling speed, he had jerked his right-hand Colt, cocked it, and pressed the trigger. The gun roared, roared again and then a third time as Gregg rolled the hammer, swinging the long barrel as he sent lead blasting into the line of figures. Before he had exhausted the load in the gun the other cowboys had joined in, snatching at their weapons and sending a hail of lead towards the line of horsemen.

Five of the jayhawks, the leader among them, toppled from their saddles beneath the deadly shooting of the big man. Gregg slipped his empty gun into its holster, jerked his left-hand gun, threw it into his right hand in the amazingly swift border shift, then spurred to one side, emptied his Colt, snatched the rifle from its scabbard and flung himself from the saddle.

The jayhawks struck back.

Lead whined above him as the

disorganised outlaws tried to cut down the cowboys. They still had superior numbers, and as guns blasted towards each other almost it seemed as if they could yet win the battle. Powder smoke rose in a heavy black cloud, and the screams of wounded horses and the yelling of wounded men filled the air, rising above the steady roar of Colts.

Then the hidden marksmen opened fire.

Their first volley cut down eight jayhawks. Their second six more, then they fired at will, levering their Winchesters and slamming hot lead into the milling mass of men. Caught between two fires, their ranks dwindling beneath the murderous cross-fire from the hidden riflemen, their boastful courage vanishing as they faced grim, tough cowboys with both the will and the ability to shoot and shoot to kill, they broke.

They turned, throwing down their guns and racing from the valley. To reach safety they had to pass the marksmen and as they came abreast of the hidden sharp-shooters they toppled from their saddles as though riding into an invisible wall. Gregg, crouched in the grass, his rifle at his cheek, aimed and fired, loaded, aimed and fired and kept on firing until the magazine was empty.

And then it was all over.

The gunfire died, the shouts and screams and thunder of hooves and, except for the moans of the wounded and the threshing of injured horses, the valley grew quiet.

'We got them!' Mike, his hair rumpled, his clothing soiled and dirty from where he had hugged the ground, came towards the big man. 'We got the swine!'

'Yes.'

'Like shooting fish in a barrel,' said Red. He limped as he walked, a bullet had torn the heel from one of his boots and a thin trail of blood ran down from beneath his hair where he had received a scalp wound. 'I guess that particular bunch of jayhawks won't be bothering anyone again.'

'No.' Gregg stared down the valley to where the riflemen, now on their feet, came walking towards the main body. 'Tell the men to reload and get their horses,' he snapped. 'We've got work to do.'

Quickly he reloaded his own weapons, slipping cartridges into the magazine of his rifle, opening the side gates of his revolvers, ejecting the spent cases and refilling the chambers from the cartridges carried in his belt. Fully armed once more he mounted his horse, put the rifle in its scabbard and shouted for Curly.

'What is it, Gregg?' The squat man had a torn shirt and a powder-blackened face, but was otherwise unharmed.

'Take two men and go and shoot those injured horses. Drag the wounded jayhawks to one side of the trail, we don't want them trampled, then report back to me.' Gregg waited until the scout had collected his men and ridden off. 'Losses, Red?'

'Two men dead, three wounded, none seriously.' Red stared at the shambles ahead of them and looked baffled. 'Fifty of them and we cut them down with so little loss. I'll bet that we knocked more than forty of them from their saddles.'

'Forty-six,' said Gregg. 'Five got away.' He smiled at the foreman's expression. 'I counted them while we were talking,' he explained. 'And I counted those who rode out of the valley. Not a bad result for untrained men.'

'Better than you could have done with regular troops?'

'Yes,' admitted the big man. 'These cowboys are quick on the draw and can shoot. Still, we had things all our way. The jayhawks were careless. They stood in easy line and none of them had a gun out. They underestimated us, and when we cut loose were immediately disorganized. When they returned our fire they shot wild. We merely smashed them with a storm of lead. I'm not proud of what we've done.'

'It was a battle,' said Red. 'You said so yourself.'

'It was a massacre.'

'Maybe, but it was them or us.' Red wiped his face, stared at the blood on his hand, then gingerly felt his scalp. 'I'm hurt! What do you know!' In the excitement of the battle he hadn't noticed his injury.

'You'll live.' Gregg rose in his stirrups and stared to where Curly and the other men were clearing the trail. 'Hurry it up,' he shouted to them. 'Let's get moving.'

'Just finishing.' The squat man rode up, his big hand full of gold watches. 'Look what we've found! I guess those jayhawks won't need a watch where they're going, heat's liable to melt the metal.' He chuckled as he examined his loot. 'You need a watch, Gregg?'

'Why not?' The big man accepted an ornate timepiece. He opened the case and stared inside. 'To Major Renfrew,' he read, 'with true affection from the men of his command.' He closed the watch and examined the chasing. Against a background of cannon, sabres, swords and rifles, the stars and bars of the Confederate Banner were unmistakable. He wondered what had happened to the original owner of the watch.

'You can't keep that watch, Gregg.' Mike stared distastefully after Curly as the squat man handed out his prizes to the others.

'No?' Gregg slipped the watch into his pocket. 'Why not?'

'You can't rob the dead.'

'You still haven't answered my question.'

'If you don't know then I can't tell you,' said Mike. He stared at the big man, remembering the way he had cut loose with his guns, the way he had operated on the infected wound, his grim resolve to press northwards at all costs. 'You're a hard man, Gregg. Very hard.'

'Maybe.' Gregg swung in his saddle, lifted his arm, yelled and then brought his arm sharply downwards. It was the signal to get moving, and as the cowboys obeyed, the walls of the valley echoed to their shrill yells as they encouraged the cattle to move. Slowly at first, like a rain-swollen river, the brown horde began to press towards the narrow part of the valley and the tempting grass beyond.

They surged to where the dead men and dead horses rested on the grass. They pressed on over them, and twenty thousand sharp hooves trod and pressed the mangled remains into the dirt of the valley. When they had passed nothing remained of the fierce conflict but trampled soil and scraps of leather, patches of dark moisture and shredded flesh. On the side of the valley the wounded jayhawks stared with pain-filled eyes at the riders as they passed.

One of them called to Gregg as he rode with Mike and Red.

'Hey, ain't you going to take us with you?'

Gregg didn't answer.

'You can't leave us like this,' the man called. 'We've no horses, no water, no food. Night's coming and we'll die unless you help us.'

Still Gregg didn't reply. Mike stared at his set face, then at Red. The Texans were hard, but like most hard men they could be gentle.

'We could leave them some supplies,' said Mike. 'A sack of flour and some bacon, maybe?'

'No.' Gregg didn't elaborate.

'Wait!' called the wounded man. 'Don't leave us like this. Jeff's dying and I can't move. You can't treat us as if we were animals.'

'He's right,' said Red. 'Can't we do something for them?'

'We could kill them,' said Gregg. 'Other than that, no.'

'But — '

'Why waste your pity on them?' Gregg stared at the others and his voice became harsh. 'Have you forgotten so soon? You didn't see the dead woman and the dying man. I did. Those jayhawks are getting what they deserve. If their friends want to come back for them then they'll be all right. If not then they must make out as best they can.'

'It's murder,' said Red slowly. 'I don't like it.'

'It's war,' snapped Gregg. 'They called the turn and they lost out. Now they must pay for it. Do you think they would have worried about us? They would have shot us down and left us to rot. To hell with them.'

Mike glanced at Red and nodded. Red reined, dropped back, took a canteen of water and a small sack of flour from one of the chuck wagons and dropped the supplies near the wounded men. He rode back, ready for an argument, but Gregg didn't argue. He didn't look back, either.

He was, as Mike had said, a hard man.

6

Colorado and the great ramparts of the Rockies looming far to the west. The soil was turning arid, dry, merging into desert, but because it was the trail the lowing herd moved slowly over the stony ground. Outriders had watched for further signs of the jayhawk menace, but had long lost the fear of being taken and pursued. Now the immediate threat was from the actual terrain, not the human wolves who roved the borders. Mike spoke about it at camp one night, sitting before the fire, sipping his coffee and listening to the thin, plaintive voices of the night guards as they watched over the sleeping cattle.

'We're heading for trouble, Gregg,' he warned. 'We've got to find water soon and some good grass. Cows can't live in the desert.'

'I know it.' Gregg slumped a little as

he sat before the fire. He had ridden far that day, roving far ahead to find easy passage for the cattle. He had returned to camp and Curly had taken over and was now far to the north. The squat man had proved himself to be an excellent scout, and both he and Gregg took turns at riding far-point.

'Did you spot water, Gregg?' Red helped himself to coffee. 'Even the water barrels on the chuck wagons are getting low.'

'We'll reach the Pueblo in a couple of days,' said Gregg. 'There's water and feed there and we can rest up for a couple of days.' He rubbed at his chin, frowning at the stubble which coated lips and jaw. 'I'm not worried about the water.'

'Glad someone's happy,' said Red. He sipped at his coffee, put down the empty cup, built himself a cigarette.

'What are you worried about, Gregg?' Mike was shrewd and he had noticed the increasing restlessness in the big man during the past few days. 'You spot anything ahead?'

'No.'

'You sure, Gregg?'

'I'd tell you if I did. There's nothing to worry you.'

'Maybe not.' Mike took a cigar from his pocket, lit, it, breathed smoke. 'This part of the country's new to me. As far as I know no one has yet blazed a trail through here. The Indian Nations are something which no man knows much about.' He paused, looking at the tip of his cigar. 'Is that it, Gregg?'

'What?'

'Indians?'

'Maybe.' Gregg stared into the fire. 'This is Indian country and the Sioux don't like settlers passing through.'

'We ain't settlers.'

'We're white men,' said Gregg. 'To an Indian that's enough.'

'We can handle the Indians,' said Red confidently. 'One white man's worth twenty of those red savages. Let them all come, I ain't afraid.'

'I'm not worried about you,' said

Gregg. 'I'm worried about what the Indians may do to the cattle. This is bad country, full of gullies and covered with rocks. A stampede here would cost us a deal in maimed and dead steers.'

'I see.' Mike nodded, he had seen the effects of stampeding cattle before. He stretched and stared up at the sky. The night was clear, moonless, and the stars glittered like a double-handful of diamonds scattered by some careless jeweller across the vault of heaven. It was peaceful, strangely so, and it was hard to believe that anything could harm them in this perfect quiet.

'I'll ride ahead again tomorrow,' said Gregg. 'You keep the herd moving along the trail we've marked. If I spot anything I'll let you know.' He rose and moved towards his blankets. 'Sleep easy.'

He settled down, his head resting on his saddle, easing his tired body. He was in the saddle almost fifteen hours a day, had been since they started, and tough as he was the strain was telling on him.

For he wasn't riding like the rest of the cowboys, as the trail-finder he had to rove far ahead and to either side, searching for the easiest path for the cattle to follow. It wasn't an easy job. A mistake could cost them lost steers and wasted days while they backtracked and tried again, and the easiest path wasn't always the right one.

One consolation was that once the trail had been blazed others could follow with little trouble.

He fell asleep dreaming of twenty million steers pounding their way over the path he had found for them.

Dawn found him in the saddle ten miles from camp. He rode easily, his eyes flickering as they swept from side to side of the route he was taking. After sun-up he dismounted, built himself a small fire and cooked a meal of coffee and johnny cakes, eating the half-raw dough with the tip of his knife. Game was scarce in this part of the country, and both men and animals were on short rations. He was kicking out the fire when he heard a hail, and Curly, followed by a couple of bearded men, came towards him.

The squat man rode his horse, the others sat on mules. They wore rough clothing and high boots of miners, each carried a pistol and both were grinning.

'Meet Joe and Sam,' said Curly. 'Boys this is Gregg, the boss.'

'Howdy.' Gregg looked at Curly.

'Me and Sam are brothers,' said Joe. 'Curly rode into our diggings last night and we got talking.' He grinned. 'Man, are we glad to see you!'

'Why?'

'Strangers are scarce in these parts,' said Sam. He jerked his thumb back towards the hills. 'Me and Joe have a small claim, some placer stuff and a thin vein of high-grade ore. We manage to pan some dust and could really strike it rich if we could work through the winter. We got fuel and blasting powder and tools, and was hoping to follow the main vein back into the rock.'

'Many of you around here?'

'Some. Most of the boys work the Leman diggings, but quite a few do some prospecting and pan a little dust from the creeks.' He looked at Gregg. 'Curly here told us that you've got plenty of beef.'

'That's right.'

'Me and the rest of the boys are starved for beef,' said. 'Care to help us out?'

'You can have a steer if you're desperate,' said Gregg. He glanced around the foothills. 'No game?'

'None that we can find,' said Joe. 'The Sioux make it unhealthy to hunt too far away from the diggings and, anyway we ain't got the time. Every hour lost at the claim means just that much paydirt we don't get. With things as they are it would pay us to hire a hunter to keep us in food.'

'Why don't you trade with the Indians for game?' Gregg hitched his thumbs in his cartridge belt. 'Treat them fair and they won't rob you.'

'I know it.' Joe spat and rubbed his

beard. 'We ain't like most people. Me, I get on well with the Indians, leastways, I used to. Did some trading in the Nations and dealt with the Cheyenne and Comanche. Even went down to trade with the Apache one time, but that was before the trouble with the settlers.'

'Well?'

'The Sioux ain't eager to do business. We got some meat from them two, three weeks ago, and gave them some blankets and tobacco, but we're running out of supplies and the Indians aren't coming around as they used to. I guess there's trouble brewing. These settlers can't keep their fingers off a trigger when they see an Indian. Sioux, Dakota, Comanche, Cheyenne, it don't make no difference to them. The way they talk you'd think that the only good Indian was a dead one.'

'I've heard a lot of people say that,' said Gregg. 'Don't you agree with it?'

'No.' Sam glanced at his brother. 'Joe and me reckon that an Indian's the same as anyone else. Treat them fair and they'll treat you fair. We ain't never had no trouble.' He shrugged. 'Had a couple of horses stole one time, but fixed that. We use mules, and the Indians don't go for mules.'

'It still don't pay to trust them,' said Curly. He touched his hat. 'I should know.'

'Maybe, but this country is big enough for the both of us.' Joe wet his lips. 'You against them, mister?'

'I've fought the Indians,' said Gregg. 'Traded with them too a little. They aren't like us and it's a mistake to think so. Left alone and treated fair they'll act human. The trouble is no one leaves them alone. Traders swap whiskey for furs and gold. The traders sell them rifles, and the guns, together with the rotgut, sends them crazy. Indians shouldn't drink, they can't take it, and when they've got a skinful they go on the warpath.'

'Sure,' said Sam uneasily. 'We know that.'

'When they are on the prod they don't care for white men being friendly towards them,' said Gregg. 'My uncle learned that the hard way. He treated them right, fed them in winter, traded fair. Then one day they got hold of some firewater and went on the warpath. My uncle got killed by the very Indians he'd befriended. They took his hair and burned his cabin. It happened during the war.'

'So there's bad Indians,' said Joe. 'So what? We mind our business and don't want trouble.'

'You may get it without asking,' said Curly. 'You be careful.'

'We'll be careful,' promised Sam. He looked at Gregg. 'You talk like a man who knows both sides. What do you think?'

'I think that the Indians should be given lands and left alone,' said Gregg. 'They have their own way of life, and it isn't ours. We should treat our own people as we treat the Indians. I'd like to see every trader selling them whiskey

131

put up against a tree and shot. I'd like to see every trader who gives repeating rifles and ammunition treated the same. Then we should stop killing the buffalo, stay away from their reservations and leave them to work out their own destiny.'

'They have got reservations,' said Curly. 'You know they have.'

'Sure.' Gregg sounded bitter. 'We gave them lands they had ridden and hunted for generations. We came in and told them that their lands didn't belong to them, but that we would give them a little to call their own. All right, we did that and then what happened? We started to rob them of the very lands we had given them. Settlers moved in and there was trouble. Peace was made, new treaties were signed and the same trouble started. Gold was found in the Black Hills and the Dakotas had to go to war to stop the miners ruining their land. The miners were backed by the cavalry and so the Indians lost again. They always lose, they always will and it's men like these two who cause most of the trouble.'

'That ain't fair,' said Sam. 'Me and Joe treat them right.'

'Maybe you do, and that's to your credit, but you're still in their lands digging out their gold.'

'So what? They don't want it. Indians have no use for gold.'

'Not now they haven't, but maybe they will later. Anyway that's not the point. This is Sioux country and you're in it. You've found gold in the hills and you know what happens when gold is found. You'll start a gold-rush, the wagons and miners will stream into the Indian Nations, the settlers will follow them and then there'll be another uprising. So the cavalry move in to keep peace, there'll be an Indian war and lots of people will get killed, and after it's all over the Sioux will be driven back even further. So it goes on and it won't end until the Indian has been wiped out.'

'Maybe.' Joe looked thoughtful. 'But what can we do about it? Moving out won't stop the others and, anyway, we may as well take the gold as anyone else. Hell, we've worked hard enough for it.'

'I know.' Gregg shook his head and stared about the countryside. 'Seen any signs of Indian trouble lately?'

'No, just that they don't come trading no more and we're scraping the bottom of the flour barrel.' Joe cleared his throat. 'Look, mister, we've got a proposition to make. Can you sell us some steers?'

'I think so.' Gregg looked at the prospector. 'How many?'

'Say a hundred head.'

'A hundred!'

'That's right.' Joe spat and wiped his mouth on the back of his hand. 'This is the position. Me and Sam and the others want to work through the winter. Normally we'd have to pull out and go for supplies or have them delivered to us. Both ways costs plenty. Freight is high in these parts and deliveries take too long. We hoped that the Indians would keep us supplied, but we're running out of trade goods. So we've either got to move into town for the winter or pay through the nose for what food any cheating contractor wants to send us. If we move into town or go for supplies ourselves it will take too long and we lose the chance of getting extra gold.'

'Those hills must be heavy with pay-dirt,' said Curly. 'I've a mind to have a crack of prospecting myself.'

'You're welcome,' said Sam. He looked at Gregg. 'In the spring the rush will start, we know it and we know too that when it happens we'll get squeezed out. We want to make a head start and get what gold we can while we're able. We figure that if we work through the winter we'll just about exhaust our claim, and when the spring comes we can move out and look for another strike. We might even be able to retire.'

'I get what you're driving at,' said Gregg. 'Go on.'

'We figured that if you'd sell us some

cattle we could supply ourselves and the rest of the boys with beef through the winter,' said Sam. 'A hundred head would just about do it.' He stared at the big man. 'We'll give you twenty dollars a head in dust. You deliver them to the diggings, Curly knows where they are.'

'I see.' Gregg sat on his horse and stared at the prospectors. He knew quite well that he was looking at a pair of opportunists and had discounted all they had said about the Sioux as nothing but lies. These men were too hard, too greedy, for any sentiment to trouble them when dealing with the Indians. The Sioux probably had stopped trading with them because they were being cheated. Sam and Joe had met Curly and seen the opportunity to clear a quick profit.

Most gold camps suffered from the fact that too many men were trying to get all the gold they could as fast as they could, and no one worried about the food supply. Normally, professional hunters earned a good living by supplying such camps with fresh meat, and a few contractors made fortunes by risking the long and difficult haul with flour, beans, whiskey, clothing and other supplies, selling their wares for leather bags of gold dust at so much the ounce.

The Leman diggings was obviously a case in point. The threat of Indians had kept the normal contractors away or perhaps they had tried to make the journey, only to be attacked and killed by the Sioux. The hunters had given up, the game was scarce and the country-side unsuitable for deer, turkeys, buffalo and other easily-shot meat. The miners, greedy for gold, had waited until winter was almost upon them before worrying about supplies, and were now in the position of having to leave camp, with resultant loss of earnings, or paying high prices to anyone who could supply them with food.

Gregg knew that the miners would rather pay dearly for food than have to give up their quest for the yellow metal, for, as Sam had pointed out, it paid them to do so.

The two men hoped to buy cattle to slaughter and sell to the camps for a big profit. To them, Gregg's advance was a golden opportunity to make money the easy way.

'Twenty dollars a head,' repeated Sam. 'Two thousand dollars in dust, cash on the nail. Is it a deal?'

'No.'

'Why not, it's a fair trade?'

'You're aiming too low,' said Gregg. 'I didn't fetch those steers all this way for nothing. Aim higher and talk fast.'

'Thirty dollars a head, that's my last word.'

'Fair enough.' Gregg turned to Curly. 'Ride over to the diggings and tell the boys we've some prime beef going for sixty dollars a head. Take orders and we'll deliver by noon day after tomorrow.'

'Hold it.' Sam swallowed and looked anxious. 'You don't want to do a thing like that. The diggings is a long way from here and you don't want to waste time.' He glanced at his brother. 'I'll talk straight. We can't use a hundred head, but the camp can. We've got some dust, not much, but enough to pay you now. Call it four thousand for the hundred head.'

'Call it forty-five hundred,' said Gregg coldly. 'Cash on the nail and you take delivery from the Pueblo. More talk and I'll raise it to fifty dollars a head. Is it a deal?'

'Sure.' Sam beamed and Gregg guessed that the brothers would still double their money at least. 'At the Pueblo, you say?'

'That's right. The cattle will reach there tomorrow. I'll send word to cut you out a hundred head and you take delivery when you pay.' Gregg leaned forward in his saddle. 'Now listen. What you make doesn't worry me, that's your business. But don't try anything smart like rustling or shooting a few head from ambush. I don't want any accidents or any trouble. Be satisfied with a straight business deal and we'll stay friends.'

'Sure,' said Sam. 'Why not?'

'Suits us,' said Joe. He looked thoughtful. 'I guess that we can buy more steers at the same price?'

'Yes. You can buy beef from us at any time, provided you can pay dust on the nail.' Gregg relaxed. 'You know, a couple of smart operators would scout around and take orders for beef before it's too late. Once the word gets around that we're here you may have competition.'

'That's right,' said Sam. He kicked at his mule. 'Come on, Joe, we've got a lot to do.'

Gregg smiled as he watched the two men ride off towards the hills. Besides him Curly spat in the dust.

'It might be an idea for me to ride around myself and see what business I can scare up,' he said thoughtfully. 'Those two act like vultures smelling dead meat.'

'Forget it,' said Gregg. 'They know the country and where to find the people. We don't. Anyway, our business is blazing a trail, not acting as traders.'

'No harm in picking up a little cash,' said Curly. 'Not when it comes easy.'

'Forget it,' said Gregg again, more sharply this time. 'We've got bigger worries. Did you see any Indian sign on your scout?'

'No.'

'You sure? No cold fires, smoke, horse droppings?'

'I know how to make a scout,' said the squat man. 'I know what to look for and how to read sign. I didn't see any.'

'All right, no need to get upset about it.'

'I ain't getting upset.'

'Yes you are.' Gregg smiled at the squat man. 'Sorry, Curly, but I guess that I'm on edge. This is a dangerous stretch of territory.'

'You should take a rest,' said Curly. 'Look, there's a town about a hundred miles from here. A boom town. Some saloons and dancing girls and a faro bank. Why not ride in and have some relaxation?'

'A town?'

'That's right.'

'Who told you about it? Joe and Sam?'

'Yes.' Curly looked at the big man. 'Why, what's wrong?'

'There isn't a town that I know of anywhere near here,' said Gregg. 'I wonder — ?'

'You think it was a trick to get us to leave the herd?'

'No.' Gregg shook his head. 'No I can't think that.' He snapped his fingers. 'I'll bet I know what they were talking about. A buffalo camp, that's what. A place where the hunters come to sell their hides and spend their money.'

'Well?' Curly looked stubborn. 'That's a town, ain't it?'

'If you can call a few tents and some whiskey wagons a town, then I suppose it is. But it won't be there now. Those buffalo camps follow the hunters and they'd be on their way south by now.' He chuckled at the expression on the squat man's face. 'Sorry, Curly, I guess you'll have to wait until we hit a real town for your spree.'

'Darn it,' said the scout. 'I was hoping to persuade you into taking a few day off. I'm so dry for whiskey that I could spit.' He smacked his lips. 'Even trade rotgut would taste fine after all that dust I've swallowed.'

'You'll have to wait,' said Gregg again. 'Ride back to the herd and tell Mike to cut out a hundred head at the Pueblo. Tell him to take gold dust to the value of forty-five hundred dollars, you know the deal. If those men want more cattle they can have them. Tell Mike to cut out the weakest head, they only want them for slaughter and they'd probably die on the trail anyway.'

'Why, Gregg?' Curly looked sharply at the big man. 'You expecting trouble?'

'Maybe.' The big man spurred his horse towards the north. 'See you later.'

Curly nodded and stood staring after Gregg until the big man had dwindled into the distance, then, sighing, he commenced the long ride back to the herd.

7

It was two weeks before Gregg returned to the camp. Two long weeks in which he had scouted far to the north, swinging wide to east and west, searching, always searching, for the trail which the cattle must take.

He had left markers, stones and sticks, marks blazed on stunted trees, ashes of fires, anything to tell the trail-wise cowboys which route to follow.

Now the herd was settled in a shallow fold between the hills. Ahead of them lay the unknown territory leading to their goal, behind them, trampled by the twenty thousand hooves, the trail they had followed was marked clearly over prairie, across rivers, winding between hills and circling desert and rocky ground.

Fires blazed on the ground, the big

cooking fires before the chuck wagons, smaller fires around which men, sleeping like logs, rested with their heads on their saddles and their feet towards the hot embers. Horses stamped and pawed the ground at their stakes, their breath pluming from their nostrils in the chill night air. Mike, wrapped in a mackinaw, rode towards the fires, slumped in his saddle, feeling the strain of pushing, ever pushing the herd northwards at the maximum rate of which they were capable.

At times like this he felt his age. He had started doing a man's work at twelve and had done ever since. His body bore the scars of old wounds, gunshots received from rustlers and outlaws, bullet wounds collected during the range wars when cattlemen had fought like madmen to lay claim to water and range. Those days were over, had been for many years now, but Mike knew, as did most Texans, that they would return.

The war had caused a truce, the

mounting herds had presented a problem and had become a headache, not an asset. But after they had left the ranges to go to the markets and money had poured into the coffers of the cattle barons, the old troubles would start again.

And this time the problem would be aggravated by the settlers, sheep-raisers, homesteaders and the thousands flooding towards the West. They wanted land did those settlers. They wanted to cut up the range and break the sod and plant crops. It would only be a matter of time before the free grass was a thing of the past.

Mike didn't like to think about it.

He swung stiffly from the saddle, stripped it from his horse, tethered the animal to the picket line and, carrying the saddle, returned to the fire. Red, sprawled in his blankets, rose as the rancher approached.

'Coffee, Mike?'

'Thanks.' The rancher accepted the tin cup, and nursing the brew sat down before the fire. He held out his hands to the small blaze, warming them, then sipped the coffee. He took out a cigar, lit it, inhaled. The warmth of the coffee and the fire, the familiar taste of tobacco, served to rid his body of some of its fatigue.

'Gregg back yet?'

'Not yet.' Red sat up, his hands clasped around his knees. Range-wise he stared at the sky, sniffed the air, looked towards the restless cattle. The sky was dark, without star or moon, overladen with cloud. There was a peculiar tension in the air, the threat of storms to come, and all the men spoke quietly, keeping their voices down to whispers and taking care to make no sharp or sudden sound.

'The herd is restless tonight,' said Mike. He listened to the thin singing of the cowboys as they rode the night watch. The men sang in soft, soothing tones, lulling the cattle and easing their fears by the sound of their presence. A nervous steer could run amok at the sight of a horseman riding out of the dark, a shadow among the shadows, the singing both advertised his coming and reassured the nervous beasts.

'They're tired,' said Red. 'Pushing them at this rate is heading for trouble.'

'Gregg wants us to move fast.'

'Sure, but what's the point? The way we're wearing them down we'll have to rest up for days, maybe weeks to get them in condition again. What's the point of covering twenty miles in a day if we have to rest up for a day afterwards? We'd be better off covering the ground at an easy ten miles a day.'

Mike nodded, not answering, then stood up as a mounted horseman came towards them. It was Gregg, and he reeled in his saddle like a man at the last stages of exhaustion. His horse too was jaded, lathered with sweat and blowing hard. The big man almost fell from the saddle.

'Have someone take care of my horse.' he said. 'I'm all in.'

'Sure,' said Mike, but he didn't move.

Gregg noticed the hesitation, grunted, and stripped the saddle from his mount. He knew the Western method of living, which stated that a man must at all times tend his horse before himself. Exhausted as he was, yet he had to make an attempt. Once made, others would take over, but no Westerner would help a man who refused to help himself. Red swore as he saw a stain on the big man's shirt.

'You hurt, Gregg?'

'Yes.' Gregg leaned against the horse, the effort of removing the saddle almost too great for him. His left shoulder burned, and as he moved he could feel the warm flow of blood along his side.

'Sit down.' Red supported him, took his horse, called to one of the cooks and gave quick orders. He returned to find Mike handing the big man a bottle of whiskey.

'Drink this,' ordered the rancher. 'You hungry?'

'Yes.' Gregg tilted the bottle and swallowed. 'Set some water to boil,

Mike. It's your turn to do the cutting.' He winced as he removed his shirt. High in his left shoulder the broken shaft of an arrow rested in the centre of a blood-smeared wound. 'Can you get this thing out?'

'Sure.' Mike stared at the arrow, touched it, stared at the big man. 'Indians?'

'Sioux.' Gregg moved his injured shoulder. 'I ran into a small party well to the north. They wore paint and were on the warpath. I got a few of them and ran for it. I collected this during the chase.'

'Did you try to get it out?'

'Yes. I left it alone when I found it was a war arrow. I'd do more damage pulling out those barbs than leaving it alone. I took a wide swing to the east so as not to lead them to the herd. That's why I'm so late.' He looked at the water set to heat. 'Ready?'

'I think so.' From his own experience Mike knew what to do. He heated his knife, sterilized it, cut at the flesh surrounding the viciously-barbed arrow head. Gregg sucked in his breath with a hiss as the rancher cut out the arrow, then relaxed as it came free.

'Now wash the wound. No need to cauterize it, it wasn't infected.' He waited until the shoulder had been tightly bandaged. 'Thanks. Now where's that food?'

'Coming up,' said Red. He took the arrow head, whistled as he examined the barbs, and looked at Gregg. 'Some arrow.'

'They don't shoot them for fun,' said Gregg. 'I was lucky.' He helped himself to more whiskey. 'Where's Curly?'

'Scouting to the east. He said he saw a smoke signal rising in the distance and he wanted to take a look at who was sending it. He's been gone a couple of days.'

Gregg nodded, making no comment. One of the cooks brought a heaped platter of beans and shredded beef, the remains of a steer killed for food. Gregg spooned up the mixture, eating with a quiet concentration which told more than words just how hungry he was. Finished, he set aside the tin plate, took another drink of whiskey and handed Mike the bottle.

'That's better. Better save this for later, we may need it.' He felt in his pockets. 'Got a smoke?'

'Cigar do?'

'Sure. I've been out of tobacco for almost a week now.'

'Try one of these.' Mike handed the big man a cigar, lit it with a splinter from the fire, waited until Gregg had drawn it into comfortable life. 'What's the position, Gregg?'

'The trail is blazed for a week ahead. We'll have to pass through a canyon and then the country opens out to grass with plenty of water. I found some snow up on the hills, winter will be early this year, and we've got to press on before it hits lower down. We can't afford to get snowed up, not if we want to save the steers we can't.'

'How about further on?'

'We've been climbing for some time now. Once we get through the canyon the trail drops to the lowlands. If we can get through and push on we'll beat the snow. We can sell beef and they can go to winter pasture.' Gregg stared at Mike. 'Did you get the gold?'

'Sure. We sold a total of a hundred and thirty head. I took a round figure of five thousand five hundred dollars in dust.' Mike grinned. 'They weren't particular so we gave them the oldest and weakest steers. We would of lost them anyway.'

'We may lose more than that,' said Gregg tightly. 'From here on the trail is going to be rough. I've scouted all over this area and the canyon is the only easy way through. If we try to by-pass it we'll lose steers like flies. The terrain has no water and the ground is broken. Once past the canyon and the way is open all the way to Cheyenne. We may be able to sell the beef to the buyers there, but if not, then we can press on to Montana. Personally I'd like to get rid of them in Wyoming.'

'Why, Gregg?'

'Once we sell them then others have got the worry,' said Gregg. 'From Cheyenne it's only an easy drive up to Montana. Anyone can handle it.'

'Then why don't we?'

'Because we want to get back to Texas.' Gregg winced at the stiffness in his shoulder. 'Once the trail is blazed anyone can follow it. We've blazed it and we should get the benefit. There's nothing to stop you riding back, beating the winter and getting another drive ready for early spring. That way you can get rid of a couple of herds instead of one.'

'Sounds reasonable,' said Red. 'We could use the money and unload the stock. We could buy more to replenish the range and make this the new trail north.'

'That won't be necessary,' said Gregg. He leaned back, the cigar between his fingers, the firelight danc-ing from the harsh lines of his face.

'The east wants beef, Texas has the beef, so the buyers will find some way to get it. At the moment the jayhawks have frightened off the cattlemen. We smashed a big bunch of them and what we did others can do. Next year, or maybe the year after, the railroad will establish a railhead further west and nearer to Texas. New trails will be blazed and long drives avoided. Business men know that the cattle punchers bring money into town, so they will be eager for your trade.'

'Nice,' said Red. 'You any idea of where these railheads will be?'

'Mid-west,' said Gregg. 'There was talk about pushing the line through to Wichita or Topeka. The lines are running that way as it is. Sooner or later someone is going to establish a railhead in Texas itself, maybe Houston or Abilene, maybe Austin or Dallas. When that happens your troubles will be over.'

'That's what you think,' said Mike. He stared into the fire. 'I've been doing a lot of thinking this trip,' he said.

'Riding night guard gives a man a lot of time for thinking. I came to Texas when a man could take what he wanted and hold it just as long as he could defend it. Those days are over. We've got the ranches and we share the grass and water, but already trouble is stirring. Too many head of cattle for too little water and grass. The big outfits are squeezing out the little ones. They just send in their steers and they take over. At round-up time they grab all the mavericks.' He shrugged. 'There's been talk of lynchings and hiring gunmen. You know what that can lead to.'

'Range war,' said Gregg.

'That's right.'

'We've got other things to worry about,' said Red. 'We can handle our own kind. It's the settlers and sheep farmers who are causing all the grief. Those damn woollies chew the roots of the grass and leave the prairies bare. Without grass the steers can't live. To me it's choice of sheep or cows, we can't have both and we aren't going to.'

'And you are a cattleman,' said Gregg softly. 'You have no choice as to which to keep.'

'That's right,' said Red. 'The steers stay, the sheep go.' He grinned, a smile without humour. 'They can go peaceful or they can argue about it, but in any case they go. They go and they don't come back.'

'The common enemy,' said Gregg. 'So you kill the farmers and drive them off the range. Will that solve your problems?'

'Sure, why not?'

'Mike has already told you. Unless a man has land and grass he can call his own then he can't rest easy. He's got to get more cows, more riders, more guns to protect what he holds. Then comes a range war and men get killed. Rustlers step in and rob the herds. There's only one finish to a setup like that, and it's a bad ending for any man to have to face.'

'But what can we do about it?' Mike stared to where the cattle rested beneath a sullen sky. 'Where will it all end?'

'I'll tell you,' said Gregg softly. 'It will end with barbed wire. You'll have to fence the range.'

'No!' Both Red and Mike almost shouted the protest. They had been born to the concept of free grass and they couldn't rid themselves of it. To them, as to many like them, fencing the ranges meant the end of all they stood for.

'Why not? You'll get clear title to your land and the grass and water will be yours. You can improve your breeds without the danger of scrub bulls weakening your stock. You can adjust the size of your herds to the grass you have for them. You'll have no trouble with mavericks, the unbranded calves on your land will belong to you. What can you lose?'

'Plenty.' Red was flushed with anger. 'We can lose the freedom of the range. The prairie is ours, all of it, and we want to use it all, not just a part. Fence the range and you ruin the cattlemen.'

'I'm not arguing,' said Gregg. 'I'm not a rancher and I'm not worried either way, but it'll come. The range will be fenced just as sure as death and taxes, and if you're smart you'll get in first.'

'Maybe.' Mike scowled at the fire. The big man had talked in a way which even the rancher, bigoted as he was, recognized as cold sense. He looked up as a drop of rain fell on the fire, causing it to hiss and splutter. 'I sure hope we don't get a storm.'

'The clouds are full of rain,' said Gregg. He pulled on his mackinaw.

'I'm not so worried about the rain,' said Mike. 'I'm scared of thunder.' He listened to the lowing of the restless cattle. 'The herd's been pushed too far too fast. The steers are worn and jumpy. They are mostly bone and hide and they're getting mean.'

He paused, not needing to say more. Everyone knew how nervous steers could get when tired and hungry. They had been driven to the limit and had suffered for it. The plump cows had dwindled to thin, gaunt-looking steers, and hunger and fatigue made them awkward to handle. A sudden noise, a fright, and for no other reason than that they would rise and run away from the noise in a stampede which would carry everything before it. They would run until exhausted, hurting themselves, breaking legs, even running over the edges of cliffs to their destruction. A stampede was the one thing every cowpuncher dreaded most of all.

Mike rose, tightening his mackinaw. 'I guess that I'll ride around some more,' he said. 'You'd better saddle up too, Red, the more men we've got on the job the better it will be.' He turned and cursed one of the cooks allowing a metal billy to ring against a cook-pot. 'Watch it,' he said, yet remembering to keep his voice down. 'If you can't work in silence then don't work at all.'

The cook grunted, but took care not to repeat the incident. Lightning flashed far towards the west and a soft, almost inaudible rumble of thunder stirred the air. Again the lightning and again the thunder. Several steers rose to their feet, their eyes wild and glistening in the firelight.

'The storm's a long way off,' said Gregg. 'Over the hills. It won't trouble us.'

Mike nodded and went to fetch his horse. He put one foot in the stirrup, mounted, waited for Red to join him.

'Better bed down, Gregg,' he said. 'You're tuckered out and that wound needs rest. Get some sleep ready for the morning.'

'Sure,' said Gregg. 'I — '

He paused, a man carved from stone, and in that moment lightning flared and thunder rolled like the playing of celestial dice.

But the thunder came too late to drown out the sound which caused the big man to become suddenly rigid.

The ululating war-whoop of an Indian on the warpath.

It was followed by the crackle of shots.

Gregg rose, his tiredness and wound forgotten, and lifting his saddle he ran to the picket line. Behind him Mike was cursing in a desperate frenzy as the roar of guns echoed across the lowing herd.

'The cattle! Those damn fools will start a stampede!' He spurred forward, yelling for the men to stop firing, then swore again as the shrilling yell of the Indian drowned out his voice.

Gregg wasn't listening. His fingers raced as he tightened straps and adjusted the traces. He mounted and rode towards the sound of Mike's voice. Before them, like an angry sea, the restless cattle surged to their feet and stood sniffing at the damp air.

'Circle!' yelled Mike. 'Circle, damn your eyes. Circle!'

The cowboys knew what to do without orders, but doing it was something else. The night was dark, the cattle a blur of deep darkness relieved by the glint of an eye or horn in the distant fire-light. It was hard to ride around the steers ready and watchful for a sudden move, trying to anticipate it and ready to scare the cattle back again. They would yell and scream and fire guns and hope and pray that the leaders of the stampede would turn in a tight circle so that the herd would run around and around until milled into an immobile mass. Then the tired beasts would calm themselves and the danger would be over.

But to do all that was always hard. Without light it was impossible.

Gregg realized that. He sat his horse, not moving, his eyes weighing the chances. Turning he snapped orders to the cooks.

'Get sacks, cloth, underbrush, anything. Tie them, in bundles, fasten them to ropes, soak them in grease and set fire to them. Hurry!'

He snatched at a man as he passed.

'Get some men and horses and report back here. Fast!'

While waiting he helped the cook

prepare the improvised flares. Lashing the old sacks, dipping them in grease, tying pieces of hide and fat to the bundles to make them burn. As each rider came up to report he handed him the end of a rope.

'Set light to the bundle and ride in a circle around the herd. The flares will give us light and scare the leaders back. Move!'

The men understood and galloped off to carry out the task. A line of fire began to surround the restless cattle. A wavering, bobbing line of smoking flame, as the riders, spurring their mounts, dragged the burning bundles behind them. There was no wind and all the cattle could see was the dancing ring of flame. Terrified they shrank back into themselves, forming a milling circle surrounded by sweating cowpunchers and rearing horses.

Once the herd almost broke free. Once the steers began to thunder towards the west, to the foothills and gullies waiting to smash their legs and destroy them. Mike saw the danger and, regardless of his own safety, rode directly before the leaders, shouting, firing his Colts, screaming, making any and every noise he could think of to scare them back. Gregg joined him, two flaring bundles trailing behind him, and the noise and the sight of the flames drove back the steers.

'We've done it!' Mike, his voice hoarse, stared at the restless beasts. 'We've got them under control.'

'Maybe.' Gregg was curt. His every bone ached and his head swam from exhaustion, but he forced himself to send back for more flares, more riders to surround the cattle and fence them in with controlled flame. 'We can't dare relax. Once they break away we'll be ridden down and trampled. It'll mean the end of the drive.'

'I know it — ' Mike galloped away to give fresh instructions.

All the remainder of the night Gregg kept his riders busy with their flares. Every cowboy on the drive was mounted and at his post. The cooks worked like slaves to prepare the flares, using precious sacks, clothing, blankets, anything and everything which would burn. No one rested until the first pale light of dawn showed in the east, and then tiredly, the danger over, the cowboys trooped back to the camp.

The cooks turned their efforts to the preparation of food and coffee, and great pots of the scalding brew were drunk as tired cowboys sought to get the chill and fatigue from their bones.

It was only after they had eaten and drunk that Mike remembered the cause of the trouble.

'Who fired those shots?' he demanded. 'And why?'

'I did.' A blackened cowboy stepped forward. 'I was riding on the east when I heard the Indian yell. I saw a couple of shapes coming towards me. It was dark, too dark to make out much, but they smelt of Indians. They yelled and began firing. They didn't aim at me, but at something ahead of them. I cut loose, guess it was habit, then they yelled again and rode off.' He shrugged. 'Lucky for us they did. Had they attacked we'd have lost our hair and steers both.'

'Indians don't attack at night,' said Mike. 'They might try to steal some horses or collect a scalp, but they don't ride in yelling and firing their guns.' He looked at the cowboy. 'Are you certain they were Indians?'

'No. It was too dark to see. But they sure smelt like them.'

Mike nodded, his face thoughtful, then looked up as Gregg came riding towards him. The big man had something before him on his saddle. He stopped, dismounted, lifted down his burden.

'This is what caused the trouble,' he said tightly. 'He was on the run and some Indians chased him. He almost made it at that.' He stared down at the man he had carried.

It was Curly, and he was dead.

8

It grew dry, and the cloud of dust which marked the passage of the herd rose like a sullen pall over the nodding heads of the weary beasts. They lowed as they moved, their nostrils smelling for the water they craved, the water and the lush grass they needed to restore the fat on their bones. Hunger and weariness had made them savage, and more than once a bull would lash out with his long horns at a passing rider. Both cowpunchers and cow-ponies were too wise to be caught that way, but the sullen air of brooding discomfort mounted as the days crawled past, and men rode with watchful eyes and haunted faces, cutting their rest to a minimum as they tried to control the five thousand unpredictable animals.

And the Indians were watching.

Gregg knew it, Mike knew it, every

man who rode the trail knew it. They knew it without ever seeing sight of a painted face or mounted warrior. They knew it by the spiralling columns of smoke which rose to the clear bowl of the sky, the signs left by the side of the trail, the mounting air of tension.

Gregg rode now with the rancher and the foreman. He had blazed the trail up to the canyon ahead, and beyond that was open country to the town of Cheyenne and the rolling hills of Wyoming.

There they would sell the cattle and be free to return home. But first they had to get there.

'Bad luck Curly getting killed,' said Mike thoughtfully. 'You reckon the Sioux are after the cattle?'

'That or just because they don't like us coming into their country.' Gregg shifted in his saddle, his eyes flickering over the rising hills to either side. They were getting close to the canyon.

'You think they will attack?' Red

sounded hopeful. 'Maybe they just want to watch us?'

'They didn't want to watch Curly.' Gregg frowned at the trail ahead. 'I don't like it. I'd say that Curly stumbled on a big war-party and they chased him to close his mouth. They closed his mouth all right, but that won't help them. We know they are around somewhere and we know what to expect. Sioux are mean fighters and they mean business.'

'Couldn't we trade with them?' Red shifted the guns at his waist. 'Maybe we could give them some blankets and things to let us through. Seems that they might do themselves a deal that way. Cattle are no good to Indians.'

'They are good for white men,' said Gregg. 'With this beef the settlers can raise stock or trade it to the east for rifles and ammunition. Or the buyers will spread the word and other herds will be driven up this trail. Either way the Indians stand to lose, and they know it. I don't figure that the Sioux would be interested in a few blankets or trade goods. They want our hair.'

'They'll have trouble getting mine,' said Red. 'I don't figure to go out without making them pay for it.'

'If we knew where they were it wouldn't be so bad,' said Mike. 'It's this waiting and watching and never seeing anything which is so bad. I'm getting to feel that the quicker they attack the better. At least we'd know what was happening.'

'They'll attack soon enough,' said Gregg. 'I'm hoping that they wait just a little bit too long.'

'How do you mean?'

'You'll see.' Gregg took the rifle from its scabbard, levered a fresh shell into the chamber, replaced the bullet he had evicted and replaced the rifle. From each holster he took one of the long-barrelled Colts, opened the side gate, spun the cylinder and checked the loading. Satisfied, he slipped the guns back into their holsters, took up his reins and turned the horse from the trail.

'Where are you going?' Mike stared anxiously at the big man.

'Reckon I'll make a small scout,' said Gregg. 'I want to know just what we're up against. You keep driving the herd and don't let them have any water.'

'No water?' Mike looked puzzled. 'Why?'

'You heard what I said.' Gregg nodded and rode towards the hills on his right. He rode openly, knowing that in all probability sharp eyes were studying his every move. That was a chance he had to take.

At the summit of the hill, just before he crossed the skyline, he halted and stared back at the herd. The rising cloud of dust obscured all detail, but he could see the rolling tide of brown bodies as the steers surged forward. Behind them rolled the chuck wagons, much closer to the tail of the herd than normal, and all around the cows and wagons the cowpunchers rode with their hands never far from their guns and their eyes watchful.

Gregg studied them for a long moment, his eyes thoughtful, then abruptly he spurred his mount and rode into the hills.

It was a chance he was taking, a desperate chance. He could be found and captured and put to death either quickly or by torture. He could be seen and engaged in a running fight, only to die as Curly had died. Or he could pit his skill and wits against those of the Indians and hope to learn something of their numbers and intentions. One thing he knew, to proceed without such information was asking for certain trouble.

He lost sight of the herd as he rode deeper into the hills. He rode with caution, his eyes flickering from side to side, watchful for Indian sign. A defile led into the hills and he followed it, staring at the stony ground. He reined, dismounted and stared at a little pile of horse droppings. They were fresh and moist, showing that a rider had passed this way within the past hour. Grimly Gregg mounted and rode slowly on his way.

He saw nothing. He twisted and traversed and climbed higher into the hills, but it was only when he was far from the herd that he spotted his first Indian.

It was a warrior, painted and bedecked with feathers, sitting astride his pony on a high bluff. Gregg dismounted as he saw him, leading his horse into a small canyon and tethering the animal to a stunted bush. Taking the Winchester from its scabbard he made his way cautiously on foot towards the Indian sentinel.

The warrior had not seen him, or if he had he made no sign. Gregg wormed his way closer, blending with the rocks, staying in cover, his eyes narrowed as he surveyed his chances. Where there was one Indian the possibility was high that there would be more. If they caught him then Gregg knew that they would kill him and take his scalp as a trophy with as little hesitation as he would kill a sidewinder and take its rattles as a memento.

The bluff on which he had seen the Indian was the nearest edge of a shallow cup cradled in the hills, a natural camping ground and assembly place. Gregg worked his way towards the edge, holding his rifle so that it would not strike against the rocks, and when he had reached the lip stared down into the hollow.

He stared at almost three hundred Indians.

A complete village rested in the hollow. The painted tepees stood in a wide circle around a central fire, the smoke from which rose in a hazy plume towards the sky. Dogs and horses, squaws and children, old men and young braves, it was a complete village. Why they were in the hills instead of being out on the plains Gregg had no idea. It could have been that they were on the move from one hunting ground to another or, as was likely, on the run from the cavalry. Whatever the reason, Gregg knew that they meant trouble.

He could tell that from the way the warriors were dressed. They wore paint, their faces coloured with red and vermilion, orange and black into grotesque masks designed to frighten the enemy. They carried lances and tomahawks, bows and arrows, and some of them had rifles. A few carried shields, the symbolic shields made of buffalo hide thick enough to turn a pistol bullet at long range. The few warriors who carried them did not do so for protection. They believed that the shields granted them spiritual protection against their enemies, and only a warrior of proved courage was permitted to own such a shield. In a way it was the same with the feathers in their hair. A warrior gained a feather by means of a coup. It signified an individual act of bravery and was not lightly won. A feather was granted when a warrior was the first to ride into battle and touch an enemy with his bare hand. Or because he had crept into an enemy encampment at night and returned with a scalp. Warriors with many feathers were held in high regard by their companions as having shown that they were men of great valour, and it was the ambition of every Indian boy to gain such a coup as early as possible.

This desire made them reckless in the face of danger and was the reason why so many Indians had been shot while trying to perform deeds of stupid valour. Stupid to the white man, that was; to the Indians it was something quite different.

Gregg stared down into the hollow and mentally counted the warriors he could see. While he watched, a small party of mounted braves rode into the village from the further side of the hollow and appeared to be talking to the elders. A chief stepped from one of the tepees. He was an old man, but carried himself as upright as any young warrior. He wore a long, feathered head-dress, and about his waist was wound a colourful sash. The sash was looped about his body, and when unravelled would be about ten feet long. Like the shields and the coup feathers the sash was a mark of proven valour and had to be earned the hard way.

The wearer of such a sash rode into battle, dismounted, transfixed the end of the sash to the ground with his lance and then fought off all-comers. No matter how fierce the fighting he was not permitted to remove the lance and retreat. Only a friend could perform that service for him. Sash wearers among the Indians were few and far between. Gregg knew that he was staring at a chief of exceptional courage.

The chief spoke to the newcomers, gestured towards the sun, towards the direction of the cattle, then sat down. He produced a pipe, lit it from the fire, blew smoke to the north, the east, the west and south. He puffed towards the sky and towards the ground, then having done that he passed the pipe to one of the newcomers. The man accepted it, repeated the ceremonial puffing and passed it on. The visitors squatted around the fire and the pow-wow commenced.

Gregg could guess what it was all about.

The Indians had called to other villages and were even now settling plans as to how best to attack the cowpunchers.

Gregg wasn't surprised that a council meeting had been called to settle so minor a problem. The Indians were bad generals. They had no discipline and tended to act as individuals rather than as a concrete whole. They would ride alone or in small parties, stealing horses and collecting what scalps they could, but when it came to a major engagement much talk and argument was necessary before they could begin. Indians recognized no master and any allegiance they gave to their chiefs was because they respected, not feared him. They would follow a man who had proven his courage but for no other reason. They would not take or obey any order they thought was unfair, and if the chief insisted then they would leave him to go their own ways.

So it was with this engagement. The village was on the move, and it was sheer bad luck that the path of their travel had met with that of the cattle drive. A few weeks, or even days, either way and they would have passed and none been the wiser. The Indians might have spotted the cattle, almost certainly would have done, but would have hesitated to ride against armed and desperate men. The village had provided many braves thirsting for battle. The cattle the cowpunchers drove would provide hides and meat for the women and children. The cowboys carried guns desired by the warriors, and their horses were valuable prizes in themselves.

An attack was inevitable.

Gregg squinted towards the pow-wow. He was far too distant to hear what they were saying, and even if he had sat next to them he knew that he couldn't understand their language. But the signs were something else. The old chief pointed to the sky and gestured with his hands. He drew in the dust and gestured again. His meaning was plain.

Gregg sighed and began to withdraw from his dangerous position. He had learned what he had wanted to find out. The Indians were present in large numbers and they were going to attack. The thing was that the cowboys could never beat them off. Having learned all that, Gregg knew that it was time for him to return to the herd.

A slight sound behind him gave warning.

He twisted, throwing himself to one side and turned with his back against the rock and his face towards the sky. Something thudded against the ground in the place where he had been lying, and as he stared upwards he could see a painted face staring into his own.

The lance the Indian had thrown quivered in the ground, giving mute testimony as to what would have happened had not Gregg's ears caught the slight sound of a moccasin-loosened stone falling from its position. The lance would have speared him to the rocky soil like a pinned butterfly on a display panel.

Even as he thought that Gregg was in action. He jerked to his feet as the Indian sprang forward, his tomahawk flashing in the sun, his mouth open to scream his war-whoop. Gregg felt his right hand snatch the Colt from his belt and his right thumb roll back the hammer. He resisted the instinctive motion, and warding off the downward blow of the tomahawk with his left forearm he lashed at the Indian's skull with the long barrel of his pistol. He hoped to down the Indian before he could give warning. He wanted to kill and be away before other warriors, attracted by the shrilling war-whoop, could come running to join in the fray.

He failed.

His arm went numb as the handle of the tomahawk slammed against it and the barrel of his Colt cracked against the Indian's skull. Either the blow wasn't hard enough or the warrior had an exceptionally thick skull, because he staggered, stepped back, and the hills rang and echoed to his yelling warning. Even as he shrilled the horrible, fear-inducing sound he was lunging forward to resume the attack, his tomahawk a glinting wheel of silver as it swung towards Gregg's head.

The Colt bucked in his hand as he shot the Indian, stepping to one side and thumbing back the hammer with a practised gesture of smoothly co-ordinated muscles. The Indian died, a great hole blown in his chest, and before he had fallen Gregg had snatched up his rifle and was running towards his horse.

Around him, seeming to step from the very rocks themselves, Indians moved out to intercept him.

There were eight of them, Gregg counted them as he ran. Even as he counted them the rifle lifted in his hands and lead and fire spurted from its muzzle. The shot went wild, screaming from the rocks with the snarling sound of a ricocheting bullet, and he grunted as he lowered the rifle and snatched at his Colt.

A man, a running man, could not help but be a poor shot with a rifle. Gregg knew that he had wasted time and lead in trying to use the Winchester while on the run.

An arrow whispered towards him and a thrown tomahawk chipped stone from a boulder at his side. He ducked, thumbed the hammer of his Colt, and echoes rolled in the hills as he fired and fired again at the advancing shapes. An Indian, his bow raised for a shot, slumped as lead tore into his heart. Another, caught as he was about to spring from a rock, screamed and fell like a shot bird. The rest, recognizing their danger, seemed to melt as they dived for the shelter of the rocks.

Gregg wasn't fooled. The only thing which could save him now was speed and accurate shooting. Unless he reached his horse and got out of the hills fast he would be overpowered and made prisoner. Grimly he resolved never to allow that. Some Indians had the reputation of treating their prisoners with a terrible cruelty, and Gregg didn't want to take a chance.

A rifle roared to his right and splintered stone gashed his face as the Indian bullet missed him by a hair. His boots slipped and skidded as he ran down the slopes, his eyes alert and the heavy gun in his hand sending lead at every lurking shape he saw. The gun empty, he changed it for the other, tucking the rifle under his arm as he made the switch. Then the Indians rushed him.

They came with screaming war-whoops, their painted faces horrible in the sunlight, their weapons gleaming as they charged. Had they sat back and used their bows and rifles they would have shot him down, but they did not do that. They were inflamed with rage, too eager to sink their knives and tomahawks into his body, to rip his scalp from his head and carry it off as a trophy to their tepees. And so they rushed at him, six of them, all eager for the kill.

Gregg shot them down in flame and thunder.

He stood, the heavy Colt roaring in his hand as he rolled the hammer and fired so fast that the explosions seemed to merge into one. Five times he fired the pistol, sending one shot towards each Indian, then dropping the empty weapon he lifted the rifle and finished the job.

The last Indian to die almost reached him, and as lead tore into his body he flung his knife at the hated white man. It streaked towards Gregg's face and, catching the gleam of the blade in the corner of his eye, he turned just in time.

There was a deep thud and the knife, nine inches of tempered steel, quivered in the wooden stock of his rifle.

Gregg stooped and snatched up his pistol. Desperate as he was for speed he took time to load his weapons. He jerked open the side-gates, ejected the spent cartridges and thumbed fresh ones from his belt. Even as he filled the last chamber he was running again towards his horse. His respite was temporary, he knew that he would be chased again as soon as other Indians could work themselves towards him.

He felt no great pleasure at having shot down his pursuers. It was good shooting, careful shooting, the kind of shooting where a man knows his weapons and knows that he can place a bullet just where he wants it to go. A man is a big target and Gregg had not been particular as to where he had shot the Indians. Head, chest, stomach, all were equally effective. He had wanted to knock them out of action, and he had.

Rifles snarled towards him as he mounted his horse and jerked at the reins. Behind him the Indians screamed with rage and drummed their heels against their ponies' sides. The wiry animals bounded forward as they felt the signals and the Indians whooped as they neared their enemy.

Gregg rode literally for his life. He wasted no time on clever play or cunning tricks. He had shot his way clear and he wanted to stay clear. No matter how good a shot a man was, numbers always stood against him in the end. With a score of screaming warriors at his heels, firing their rifles and using their bows, Gregg wanted to get away from them and the hills which held them. He would fight if he had to, but he wanted to choose his own ground.

He found it just off the trail. It was a pair of boulders cracked and weathered. Gregg reined hard as he rode around them, dismounted, snatched the heavy Colts from their holsters and stood, a gun in each hand, waiting for the attack.

His movements through the hills had put him in advance of the herd, almost to the narrow canyon beyond which lay the grass and water of Wyoming and the easy drive to Cheyenne. Mike and Red, hearing the sound of shots, would ride forward to his rescue. Gregg hoped that he wouldn't need them, and as the first of the Indians came around the boulders he swung into action.

Horses screamed as lead tore into them, bringing them down and making a barrier against the others. Indians shrilled their war-whoop and fired their rifles at the tall, calm man, who stood, a heavy gun in each hand, and shot them down with a hail of lead. The rolling thunder of the guns died, only to be caught and echoed by others. Mike and Red and half a dozen other cowboys, their horses sweating and lathered, came galloping forward, their pistols blazing smoke and flame, and at the sight of them the Indians wheeled and rode back into the hills.

Mounting, Gregg rode towards his rescuers, reloading as he went.

'Get the cattle moving,' he ordered. 'We've got to get through the canyon and do it fast.'

'Sure.' Mike gave swift orders and then stared at the big man. 'What did you learn?'

'The Indians are going to attack in force. They will wait until the herd reaches the canyon and then ride us down. They will have warriors up among the rocks and rain lead and arrows down on us. If they have their way we'll be surrounded and trapped. Once we enter the canyon we won't be able to leave it except at either end, and they will bottle us up.'

'And you told us to get moving towards the canyon?' Mike looked annoyed. 'Where's the sense?'

'We can't stay here,' snapped Gregg. 'Now that the Indians know that we know they are here they'll ride down on us. I shot a few braves back in the hills, and the rest will be screaming for revenge. The waiting's almost over. I'm gambling that the old chief will be able to make his plan stick.' Gregg rubbed at his chin. 'He should be able to, it's a good plan.'

'I'll say it is,' said Mike. 'If they trap us in the canyon we'll be dead ducks.' He stared at Gregg. 'You sure you know what you're doing?'

'I think so.'

'I sure hope so.' The rancher didn't look any too happy. 'It's going to be bad enough steering the cows through that pass without getting ourselves shot at by a bunch of Indians. Maybe we'd better turn back.'

'Back to where?'

'A little ways down the trail. We can rest up and wait for the Indians. We could even take some of the boys and smoke them out.'

'Listen,' said Gregg. 'I've seen those Indians. There's over a hundred braves in the hills and as many more scattered about. We've got less than a couple of dozen men. Say we do get into a fight, what then? We get ourselves shot and lose the cattle.' Gregg shook his head. 'We'll do it my way.'

'What way's that?'

'We'll do just what the Indians want us to do. We'll drive the cattle through the canyon just as they expect. Only we'll do it just a little bit different to what they think. We'll go through all right, but we'll go through fast. Mighty fast. Get it?'

'No.' Mike looked stubborn. 'What you getting at, Gregg?'

Gregg sighed, his patience was running out. 'Remember a few nights ago? The time when we found Curly?'

'Sure.'

'Well, there's the answer, Mike. What almost happened once can happen again — if we want it to.'

'I get it.' Mike slapped his thigh as he thought about it. 'You think it will work?'

'That's up to you. Can you stampede the herd?'

'Easiest thing in the world. I'll get the boys at the sides and rear well out of the way and we'll start whooping and shooting and scare the daylights out of them. They're as ornery as the devil as it is, what with bad going and no water.' He stared as Gregg. 'You had this in mind all the time,' he accused. 'That's why you told me not to give them water.'

'I had some idea,' admitted Gregg. 'There's plenty of water beyond the canyon and they'll be in a hurry to reach it. Any Indian who tries to stop them is going to get himself trampled down into the dust.'

'I reckon so,' said Mike. He glanced at the hills to either side. 'When?'

'Soon now. I want to get the herd through the canyon tonight before dark. Once on the other side they can scatter and we can round them up later. Some may get themselves killed, but we can afford to lose a few head.'

Gregg shifted in his saddle and stared

towards the nearing opening of the canyon.

'All right, let's get started.'

He led the way towards the approaching cattle.

9

It was almost too easy. Beneath Gregg's orders the cowboys arranged themselves at the sides and rear of the surging cattle. The chuck wagons were already out of harm's way. The steers were already eager to break into a run; the way had been long and the water scarce. Ahead was water and lush grass and soft dirt, instead of the hard, barren ground on which they trod. And they were nervous with strain and fatigue.

Gregg waited until the steers had almost reached the entrance to the canyon. From either side of the hills mounted warriors suddenly broke, riding their ponies, screaming their war-whoops, waving their lances and hoping to throw the men and cattle into confusion. Gregg, judging his time, lifted his rifle and fired it into the air.

Immediately the air crackled with gunfire as the cowboys jerked their Colts and blazed away. They yelled, the high-pitched, screaming Rebel yell of the Confederate Army, vying with that of the Indians for sheer ferocity of sound. Men rode beside the herd waving blankets, and from the chuck wagons the cooks beat with iron spoons on empty cookpots, adding to the din.

'Move!' yelled Mike. He lifted his Colt and blasted at the sky.

'Move!' screamed Red, and his gun added to the roaring thunder.

'Move!' cried the others. 'Hi-yi-yipee-aye. Yi-yi-yipee — '

The cattle began to move.

Slowly at first, then with a mounting speed the river of brown bodies and tossing horns broke from a shambling walk to a forward lope, from a forward lope into a slow run, from a slow run into an outright gallop.

Dust rose in blinding clouds and twenty thousand sharp hooves gouged at the arid soil and, as they moved, the sound of their passing was as distant thunder.

Nothing living could withstand them. Indians, riding their mounts, slewed to a halt and raced desperately for the shelter of the hills, all thoughts as to killing and slaughter forgotten as they saw the advancing tide of nodding heads and pounding hooves, long sharp horns and massed bodies. Some were lucky and managed to gain safety. Others, terrified or thrown from their ponies, misjudging or hoping to ride the herd, vanished in a welter of trampling death.

After the cattle, hidden in the rolling clouds of dust, Gregg and the cowboys passed through the Indian lines.

There was a little shooting, but not much. A few warriors rode towards them, but were easily beaten back. It was, as Mike said that night as they sat drinking coffee before the camp fire, almost too easy to be true.

'I can't understand it,' he said. 'Why didn't they follow us?'

'They probably did,' said Gregg. 'They may have ridden after us and stolen a few head. But the fight got knocked out of them. They know that we can see them coming in this territory and that's all there is to it.'

'Sounds crazy to me,' said Red. 'White men wouldn't give up like that.'

'We're lucky that Indians don't think like white men,' said Gregg. 'If they did we would have been butchered weeks ago. As it is they've made their attack and we've beaten them off. They may steal a few head for meat and maybe rope a few of the spare horses, but we can stand that.' He helped himself to more coffee. 'Anyway, we came quite a distance.'

'Most of ten miles,' said Mike. 'Hell, I never thought those cows would stop running. it's going to be a job rounding them up tomorrow.'

'They won't be far,' said Gregg. 'They just headed for the nearest water and stayed pretty close together. They were too tired to do much running, and once they came to water, stopped where they were. You'll find them strung out along the river come daylight.'

'I hope so,' said Mike. He took a broken cigar from his pocket, frowned at it, threw away the damaged portion and lit the remainder. 'How far is Cheyenne, Gregg?'

'Not too far. After we've rounded up the herd you and I will ride into town and look up a buyer.' The big man smiled at Red. 'You'd better come too. The rest of the boys can make a slow and easy drive towards town. We want to get the steers in good condition for market.' He stretched, staring up at the sky. 'I'll be glad to see a town again. Three months is long enough to live with cows.'

'Thirty years isn't too long,' said Mike. 'I love them.'

'You can have them,' said Gregg. 'Me, I've had enough.' He looked at the rancher. 'I'm giving you warning, Mike. When we sell the cows we part company. You take your share and go back to Texas. You know the trail now and you can run up a second herd like I told you.'

'And you, Gregg?' Red smiled as he stared at the big man, and Gregg guessed that he was thinking of Grace. He smiled.

'I'm heading back home, Red. The South is in a pretty nasty mess and maybe I can do some good there. Anyway, I'm not cut out to be a nursemaid to a lot of steers, I'll leave that to people who like the job.' He looked at Red. 'And the women who like the men who like the job.'

'I know what you're getting at,' said Red. 'I ain't forgetting.'

'And don't forget that wire we spoke about,' said Gregg. 'I was talking good sense.'

'Maybe.' Mike rose and Gregg knew that he had somehow offended the rancher. 'Let's turn in. I'm all tuckered out and we want to get moving early tomorrow.'

They did.

The round-up started at dawn and the tired cowboys urged tired cattle to the main body. As Gregg had promised, the job wasn't too difficult, and before noon the round-up was complete, the final count taken and the herd moving slowly towards Cheyenne and the rich grass before them.

'Four thousand seven hundred and eighty head,' reported the foreman. 'We sold a hundred and thirty and ate some more. Not bad for a three-month drive.'

'We were lucky,' said Mike. 'We had a man with us who knew how to blaze a trail. I've followed some empty-heads who thought they could take cattle over mountains and along ledges too narrow for a goat.' He spat in the dust. 'I remember one time a few years back, it was when a man said that he knew a short route to Utah. Me and some of the others chipped in a few hundred head and took a chance. It was lucky that we played safe and only sent a few head. The fool led us right deep into the mountains and we got snowbound.'

'What happened?' Gregg was interested.

'We had to wait out the winter. There was no feed for the steers and they froze up. Not that it mattered. There was no feed or shelter for us either, so we had to kill the steers and make tents from their hides. We lived on beef for four months, and I couldn't look a steer in the face for a long time afterwards. I guess a solid meat diet don't agree with me.'

'And the trail blazer?'

'We strung him up.' The rancher was casual. 'Some of the boys reckoned that he was trying to play smart. He'd been paid in gold and one night we caught him sneaking off with half-a-dozen horses. We gave him a barrel-head trial and then stretched his neck.' He spat again. 'Not that that did us any good. We still lost the cattle.'

'Tough,' said Gregg. 'On the trail blazer, I mean.'

'Maybe.' The rancher dismissed the incident. 'When we riding to Cheyenne?'

'Start any time you like.' Gregg

stared up at the sun. 'If we leave now we should arrive in a couple of days' hard riding. You in a hurry?'

'I'd like to get my hands on some real money,' confessed the rancher. 'I won't believe that this trip has really paid off until then.' He hesitated. 'You meant what you said about leaving?'

'Yes.'

'A man knows his own business,' said the rancher. 'But if you're ever near Houston I'd take it badly if you don't pay a visit.' He stared at the big man. 'We don't talk much in Texas about how we feel. If this trip pays off you've just about saved me from ruin. You've already saved my life. I guess that you can have about anything and everything I own.'

'Yes,' said Gregg. He knew the rancher meant just what he said. He changed the subject. 'You paying off the boys in Cheyenne?'

'Sure, why not?'

'No reason. I just thought that maybe it might be an idea to save some of their money for them. Pay them usual wages and hold the rest until they get back.'

'Try that and they'd lynch me,' said Mike. 'You don't know cowboys, and that's for sure. They live rough and play hard. I'll pay them off in full and they'll go on a spree which will make history. They don't want no one to nurse them.'

'You know best.' Gregg walked to his horse and adjusted the saddle. 'We going or talking?'

'Going.' Mike gestured to Red, gave orders to his men and climbed into his saddle. Together the three men rode towards Cheyenne.

Two days' travel and they rode into the frontier town. It was a big town with shops in the streets, trading posts and a nearby fort. Three saloons were open night and day and an eating-house served meat, corn bread, local fruit and other staples. They ate, hitching their horses to the rail, and over the meal Gregg asked about cattle buyers.

'I guess that Major Blake might be interested in steers,' said the owner. He was a short, greasy-looking man whose appearance belied his native honesty. 'I could use a few head myself. Getting fresh steaks are a headache.'

'This Major Blake, he the military gent up at the fort?'

'That's right.'

'Could he buy near five thousand head?'

'Hell no!' The man stared at Gregg with new respect. 'That how many you've got?'

'Yes.'

'Then you want to see the agent for this district. John Carmody is your man. He'll be more than interested. You can find him in the Black Star Saloon.'

'Thanks.' Gregg found money and paid for the food. 'This Carmody, is he an honest man?'

'You can trust him,' said the eating-house owner. He looked directly at Gregg. 'He might try to push you, but you can trust him once he's made a deal.'

'Thanks again.' Gregg hesitated.

'Give me a straight answer. How badly are cattle needed in these parts?'

'I've been serving mule steaks for the past three weeks,' said the man. 'Does that answer your question?'

Gregg nodded.

John Carmody was a man who recognized a good thing when he saw it and was quick to take action to close a deal one way or the other. He listened to Gregg, looked at Mike and Red, let his eyes drift over their travel-stained figures and at the guns hanging from their belts. He led the way to his office, produced a bottle and glasses, and got down to essentials.

'I'm interested in your cattle,' he said. 'But on one condition. You are to sell the entire herd to me. No split herds, no side deals, no nothing like that. I buy every single head or I don't buy any. Is that clear?'

'Sure.' Gregg tilted the bottle and filled his glass. He picked it up and sipped at the whiskey. He nodded. 'Good stuff.'

'Just so as we don't make mistakes,' said Carmody, 'I'll repeat that. All or none. Right?'

'I understand.' Gregg drained his glass and refilled it from the bottle. 'Meat is scarce in town. The fort holds a lot of soldiers and they have to be fed. There are prospectors in the hills and mining camps close at hand. Those miners work like horses and can eat almost their own weight in meat every week. They will be after what we've got to sell. You figure that if you buy the entire herd they will have to pay your price or go without. Right?'

'Keep talking.'

'Do I have to?' Gregg stared at the man, his lips smiling, but his eyes hard. 'You want a monopoly. All right, so you pay for it. How much?'

'Thirty dollars a head.'

Gregg rose to his feet. 'Maybe we're wasting our time,' he said. 'With what we've got to offer we can sell slow and turn a big profit. I'm in no hurry. I can set up camp outside town and sell direct. Or I can push on to Montana.'

'If you can,' said Carmody. His face hadn't changed, but his eyes had grown veiled and secret. 'Maybe you'll run into trouble. Maybe it would be a good idea for you to take what is offered.'

'Meaning?'

'Things can happen,' said Carmody. 'Accidents for example. Stampedes, rustlers, you know the sort of thing.'

'I know,' said Gregg. He rose and kicked back his chair and stared at Carmody with eyes of ice and iron. His face had hardened, and as he stared at the other he looked savage and mean and dangerous. 'I've put all I own into that herd,' he said. 'I've helped bring it up from Texas. I've fought jayhawks and shot down men. I've ridden a thousand miles with the cattle and ten times that distance looking for a trail. I've been hunted by Indians and seen a man I liked and respected killed almost before my eyes. And you sit there and threaten me! You!'

'I wasn't meaning anything,' said Carmody. He wasn't a man to be easily afraid, but something about Gregg scared him. It did more than that, it scared the very men who had ridden with him for so long. They had never dreamed that Gregg, the smiling, patient, subdued-appearing man held such a terrible devil inside of him.

'Listen,' said Gregg. 'Listen and believe what I say. If anything happens to those steers then I'll hold you responsible. If so much as one animal gets rustled then I'll come after you and hang your hide on a nail. If you're innocent then that will be just too bad — for you.'

'Cut it out,' said Carmody. 'You came here to do business, didn't you? Well, let's get on with it.' He forced a smile. 'Can't a man haggle in this country no more?'

'Not when he uses threats to gain a bargain,' snapped Gregg. He sat down and poured himself whiskey. 'We have four thousand seven hundred and eighty prime head of range-fed cattle coming this way. They are a trifle worn because we had to push them hard, but they'll soon fatten up. Make an offer for the lot and let's get this over with.'

'Thirty-five dollars a head,' said Carmody. 'That's as much as I'll pay.'

'Make it forty and pay for a round five thousand and you can have them.' Gregg helped himself to more whiskey. 'If the price is too high say so and let's get out of here.'

'Two hundred thousand dollars.' Carmody looked thoughtful. 'It's a lot of money.'

'It's a lot of beef.'

'It's still a lot of money.'

'So it's a lot of money.' Gregg emptied his glass, his face ugly. 'So what? We didn't bring those cattle up here for a few dollars' profit. You want them or not?'

'There'll be other herds coming now that you've blazed the trail,' said Carmody shrewdly. 'Maybe I can afford to wait.'

'Maybe.' Gregg rose to his feet and jerked his head at the others. 'While you're waiting I'll contact the Major at the fort. He'll be interested in prime beef at those prices and so will most other people.' He stepped towards the door, Mike and Red reluctantly following him.

'Wait.' Carmody shrugged. 'You win. Gold or greenbacks?'

'Greenbacks will do.'

'When do you want it?'

'Half now and the rest when you take possession.' Gregg snorted at the other's hesitation. 'What the hell! You have my word and your riders can soon check up. Don't tell me that you don't know about the herd already.'

'All right,' said Carmody. 'One hundred thousand dollars down and my riders will go out with you to the herd.' He smiled. 'Just so there is no misunderstanding.'

'There won't be,' snapped Gregg. 'I'm no outlaw or sidewinder.'

'Wait outside,' said Carmody. 'Have a

211

drink at the bar, on the house, naturally. I'll bring out the money.'

Over whiskey at the bar Red wiped his forehead.

'You took a chance, Gregg. What if he hadn't called you back?'

'I knew that he would.'

'But how?'

'This is a boom town,' said Gregg. 'It's rotten with gold. You saw what I had to pay for the food, and that was for mule meat. Carmody will double his money and he knows it. He can't go wrong.'

He turned as the buyer came towards them. Carmody had a thick sheaf of bills in his hands and he passed them over.

'You'll give me a bill of sale?'

'Mike will.' Gregg counted the money, stripped off twenty thousand dollars and handed it to Mike. 'Here is my share of the expenses. Right?'

'No.' Mike shook his head. 'That's too much. Anyway, the agreement was that I should supply all we needed.'

'I'm paying my share.' Gregg thrust the money into the rancher's hand. 'I'm satisfied. I've turned ten thousand into eighty in less than four months. I'm not greedy. Don't argue,' he said as Mike started to protest. 'If you don't want it give it to Red. He can use it for what he's got in mind.'

'Quit that talk,' snapped Red. He wasn't amused.

'Why?' Gregg stared at the foreman. 'You aim to have a woman like Grace fall into your lap without fighting for her.' He looked at Mike. 'Take care of this ranny, Mike. He's your son-in-law, or he will be if he has any sense.'

'I said to quit that talk,' said Red. His hand dropped to his gun.

'Cut that!' snapped Mike. 'No gunplay here or ever.'

'You heard him,' said Gregg. He smiled. 'I know how you feel, but sometimes a man needs a boost to get him over a hurdle. Now that Mike knows what I know you'll have to do something about it.' His face hardened.

'But don't ever reach for a gun unless you aim to use it. I could have killed you where you stood, and another man might have done just that.'

'Maybe.' Red was defiant. He knew that Gregg meant well, but he was confident of his own ability to use a gun. He, like all cowboys, had grown up with a Colt and was a fantastically good shot. He also prided himself on the draw. Gregg could read what was passing through his mind. He smiled, then with a sudden blur of motion reached for his guns. He jerked them, and before anyone realised what he was doing he was rolling the hammers and blasting at the wall.

The roar of the guns died and in the following silence he reloaded his weapons.

'See what I mean?' he said quietly. 'You never know.'

'No,' said Red. 'You never know.' He was staring at the spot Gregg had used for a target. He had fired ten shots in one rolling thunder of noise and used two guns to do it. He had drawn and fired before anyone had grasped what was going on. All ten shots could be covered by a ten cent piece, and the range had been almost a hundred feet.

'Let's go,' said Carmody. He looked almost physically ill. Gregg was a gunfighter, there was no denying it, and the trader knew that the demonstration had been as much a warning to him as a lesson to the foreman.

'Sure,' said Gregg. 'Let's go.'

He led the way outside to where the horses waited and vaulted into the saddle. Two men fell in behind him, Carmody's riders, but Gregg didn't worry about them. He didn't worry about anything.

He had eighty thousand dollars in his pocket and the world was before him.

He smiled as he rode down the trail he had made.

We do hope that you have enjoyed reading this large print book.

Did you know that all of our titles are available for purchase?

We publish a wide range of high quality large print books including:
Romances, Mysteries, Classics
General Fiction
Non Fiction and Westerns

Special interest titles available in large print are:
The Little Oxford Dictionary
Music Book, Song Book
Hymn Book, Service Book

Also available from us courtesy of Oxford University Press:
Young Readers' Dictionary
(large print edition)
Young Readers' Thesaurus
(large print edition)

For further information or a free brochure, please contact us at:
Ulverscroft Large Print Books Ltd.,
The Green, Bradgate Road, Anstey,
Leicester, LE7 7FU, England.
Tel: (00 44) **0116 236 4325**
Fax: (00 44) **0116 234 0205**

LAWLESS TIMES

M. Duggan

Farmer Will Pickle's life was a peaceful one until the day his wife died and he lost his farm. Bank president Mike Herman thought it a good joke to make Will the sheriff. But things didn't go as Herman had planned. And Will, now up against plenty of enemies, found his greatest challenge was Crazy Charles. Life in lawless times forced Will to live by the rule, kill or be killed — and he was more than able to oblige.

SMOKY HILL TRAIL

Mark Falcon

When the Denver Bank threatened to repossess his family home and land, eighteen-year-old Jed Stone unwillingly became involved in a robbery with his neighbours, the four McIver brothers. The McIvers got away with the strongbox, but Jed was sentenced, under an assumed name, to five years in the Kansas Penitentiary. On his release, two women came into his life as he returned home to get his share of the hold-up money. That was when the trouble would really begin!